C6000000

D1140333

THE DEAD
OF WINTER

BIRMINGHAM LIBRARY SERVICES

DISCARD

Also by Chris Priestley

The Tales of Terror Collection

Uncle Montague's Tales of Terror
Tales of Terror from the Black Ship
Tales of Terror from the Tunnel's Mouth

* * *

Mister Creecher

THE DEAD OF WINTER

CHRIS PRIESTLEY

BLOOMSBURY

LONDON · BERLIN · NEW YORK · SYDNEY

Bloomsbury Publishing, London, Berlin, New York and Sydney

First published in Great Britain in October 2011 by Bloomsbury Publishing Plc
49–51 Bedford Square, London, WC1B 3DP

This paperback edition first published in October 2011

Text copyright © Chris Priestley 2010
Decorative illustration copyright © Chris Priestley 2010

The moral right of the author has been asserted

All rights reserved
No part of this publication may be reproduced or
transmitted by any means, electronic, mechanical, photocopying
or otherwise, without the prior permission of the publisher

A CIP catalogue record of this book is available from the British Library

ISBN 978 1 4088 0004 1

MERE GREEN

- - MAY 2015

FSC
www.fsc.org
MIX
Paper from
responsible sources
FSC® C018072

Typeset by Dorchester Typesetting Group Ltd
Printed in Great Britain by Clays Ltd, St Ives Plc, Bungay, Suffolk

1 3 5 7 9 10 8 6 4 2

www.bloomsbury.com
www.chrispriestley.blogspot.com

For Adam

PROLOGUE

My name is Michael: Michael Vyner. I'm going to tell you something of my life and of the strange events that have brought me to where I now sit, pen in hand, my heartbeat hastening at their recollection.

I hope that in the writing down of these things I will grow to understand my own story a little better and perhaps bring some comforting light to the still-dark, whispering recesses of my memory.

Horrors loom out of those shadows and my mind recoils at their approach. My God, I can still see that face – that terrible face. Those eyes! My hand clenches my pen with such strength I fear it will snap under the strain. It will take every ounce of willpower I possess to tell this tale. But tell it I must.

I had already known much hardship in my early years, but I had never before seen the horrible blackness of a soul purged of all that is good, shaped by resentment and hatred into something utterly vile and loveless. I had never known evil.

The story I am to recount may seem like the product of some fevered imagination, but the truth is the truth and all I can do is set it down as best I can, within the limits of my ability, and ask that you read it with an open mind.

If, after that, you turn away in disbelief, then I can do naught but smile and wish you well – and wish, too, that I could as easily free myself of the terrifying spectres that haunt the events I am about to relate.

So come with me now. We will walk back through time, and as the fog of the passing years rolls away we will find ourselves among the chill and weathered headstones of a large and well-stocked cemetery.

All about us are stone angels, granite obelisks and

marble urns. A sleeping stone lion guards the grave of an old soldier, a praying angel that of a beloved child. Everywhere there are the inscriptions of remembrance, of love curdled into grief.

Grand tombs and mausoleums line a curving cobbled roadway, shaded beneath tall cypress trees. A hearse stands nearby, its black-plumed horses growing impatient. It is December and the air is as damp and cold as the graves beneath our feet. The morning mist is yet to clear. Fallen leaves still litter the cobbles.

A blackbird sings gaily, oblivious to the macabre surroundings, the sound ringing round the silent cemetery, sharp and sweet in the misty vagueness. Jackdaws fly overhead and seem to call back in answer. Some way off, a new grave coldly gapes and the tiny group of mourners are walking away, leaving a boy standing alone.

The boy has cried so much over the last few days that he thinks his tears must surely have dried up for ever. Yet, as he stares down at that awful wooden box in its frightful pit, the tears come again.

There are fewer things sadder than a poorly attended funeral. When that funeral is in honour of a dear and beloved mother, then that sadness is all the more sharply felt and bitter-tasting.

As I am certain by now you have guessed, the lonesome boy by that open grave is none other than the narrator of this story.

CHAPTER ONE

I looked into that grave with as much sense of dread and despair as if I had been staring into my own. Everything I loved was in that hateful wooden box below me. I was alone now: utterly alone.

I had never known my father. He was killed when I was but a baby, one of many whose lives were ended fighting for the British Empire in the bitter dust of Afghanistan. I had no extended family. My mother and I had been everything to each other.

But my mother had never been strong, though she had borne her hardships with great courage.

She endured her illness with the same fortitude. But courage is not always enough.

These thoughts and many others taunted me beside that grave. I half considered leaping in and joining her. It seemed preferable to the dark and thorny path that lay ahead of me.

As I stood poised at the pit's edge, I heard footsteps behind me and turned to see my mother's lawyer, Mr Bentley, walking towards me accompanied by a tall, smart and expensively-dressed man. I had, of course, noticed him during the funeral and wondered who he might be. His face was long and pale, his nose large but sharply sculpted. It was a face made for the serious and mournful expression it now wore.

'Michael,' said Bentley, 'this is Mr Jerwood.'

'Master Vyner,' said the man, touching the brim of his hat. 'If I might have a quiet word.'

Bentley left us alone, endeavouring to walk backwards and stumbling over a tombstone as he rejoined his wife, who had been standing at a respectful distance. Looking at Jerwood again, I thought I recognised him.

'I'm sorry, sir,' I said, gulping back sobs and hastily brushing the tears from my cheeks. 'But do I know you?'

'We have met, Michael,' he replied, 'but you will undoubtedly have been too young to remember. May I call you Michael?' I made no reply and he smiled a half-smile, taking my silence for assent. 'Excellent. In short, Michael, you do not know me, but I know you very well.'

'Are you a friend of my mother's, sir?' I asked, puzzled at who this stranger could possibly be.

'Alas no,' he said, glancing quickly towards the grave and then back to me. 'Though I did meet your mother on several occasions, I could not say we were friends. In fact, I could not say with all honesty that your mother actually liked me. Rather, I should have to confess – if I were pressed by a judge in a court of law – that your mother actively *dis*liked me. Not that I ever let that in any way influence me in my dealings with her, and I would happily state – before the same hypothetical judge – that I held your late mother in the highest esteem.'

The stranger breathed a long sigh at the end of this speech, as if the effort of it had quite exhausted him.

'But I'm sorry, sir,' I said. 'I still do not under-stand ...'

'You do not understand who I am,' he said with a

7

smile, shaking his head. 'What a fool. Forgive me.' He removed the glove from his right hand and extended it towards me with a small bow. 'Tristan Jerwood,' he said, 'of Enderby, Pettigrew and Jerwood. I represent the interests of Sir Stephen Clarendon.'

I made no reply. I had heard this name before, of course. It was Sir Stephen whom my father had died to save in an act of bravery that drew great praise and even made the newspapers.

But I had never been able to take pride in his sacrifice. I felt angry that my father had thrown his life away to preserve that of a man I did not know. This hostility clearly showed in my face. Mr Jerwood's expression became cooler by several degrees.

'You have heard that name, I suspect?' he asked.

'I have, sir,' I replied. 'I know that he helped us after my father died. With money and so forth. I had thought that Sir Stephen might be here himself.'

Jerwood heard – as I had wanted him to hear – the note of reproach in my voice and pursed his lips, sighing a little and looking once again towards the grave.

'Your mother did not like me, Michael, as I have said,' he explained, without looking back. 'She took

Sir Stephen's money and help because she had to, for her sake and for yours, but she only ever took the barest minimum of what was offered. She was a very proud woman, Michael. I always respected that. Your mother resented the money – and her need for it – and resented me for being the intermediary. That is why she insisted on employing her own lawyer.'

Here he glanced across at Mr Bentley, who stood waiting for me by the carriage with his wife. I had been staying with the Bentleys in the days leading up to the funeral. I had met him on many occasions before, though only briefly, but they had been kind and generous. My pain was still so raw, however, that even such a tender touch served only to aggravate it.

'She was a fine woman, Michael, and you are a very lucky lad to have had her as a mother.'

Tears sprang instantly to my eyes.

'I do not feel so very lucky now, sir,' I said.

Jerwood put his hand on my shoulder. 'Now, now,' he said quietly. 'Sir Stephen has been through troubled times himself. I do not think this is the right time to speak of them, but I promise you that had they not been of such an extreme nature, he would have been at your side today.'

A tear rolled down my cheek. I shrugged his hand away.

'I thank you for coming, sir – for coming in his place,' I said coolly. I was in no mood to be comforted by some stranger whom, by his own admission, my mother did not like.

Jerwood gave his gloves a little twist as though he were wringing the neck of an imaginary chicken. Then he sighed and gave his own neck a stretch.

'Michael,' he said, 'it is my duty to inform you of some matters concerning your immediate future.'

I had naturally given this much thought myself, with increasingly depressing results. Who was I now? I was some non-person, detached from all family ties, floating free and friendless.

'Sir Stephen is now your legal guardian,' he said.

'But I thought my mother did not care for Sir Stephen or for you,' I said, taken aback a little. 'Why would she have agreed to such a thing?'

'I need not remind you that you have no one else, Michael,' said Jerwood. 'But let me assure you that your mother was in full agreement. She loved you and she knew that whatever her feelings about the matter, this was the best option.'

I looked away. He was right, of course. What choice did I have?

'You are to move schools,' said Jerwood.

'Move schools?' I said. 'Why?'

'Sir Stephen feels that St Barnabas is not quite suitable for the son – the ward, I should say – of a man such as him.'

'But I am happy where I am,' I said stiffly.

Jerwood's mouth rose almost imperceptibly at the corners.

'That is not what I have read in the letters Sir Stephen has received from the headmaster.'

I blushed a little from both embarrassment and anger at this stranger knowing about my personal affairs.

'This could be a new start for you, Michael.'

'I do not want a new start, sir,' I replied.

Jerwood let out a long breath, which rose as mist in front of his face. He turned and looked away.

'Do not fight this,' said Jerwood, as if to the trees. 'Sir Stephen has your best interests at heart, believe me. In any event, he can tell you so himself.' He turned back to face me. 'You are invited to visit him for Christmas. He is expecting you at Hawton Mere tomorrow evening.'

'Tomorrow evening?' I cried in astonishment.

'Yes,' said Jerwood. 'I shall accompany you myself. We shall catch a train from –'

'I won't go!' I snapped.

Jerwood took a deep breath and nodded at Bentley, who hurried over, rubbing his hands together and looking anxiously from my face to Jerwood's.

'Is everything settled then?' he asked, his nose having ripened to a tomato red in the meantime. 'All is well?'

Bentley was a small and rather stout gentleman who seemed unwilling to accept how stout he was. His clothes were at least one size too small for him and gave him a rather alarming appearance, as if his buttons might fly off at any moment or he himself explode with a loud pop.

This impression of over-inflation, of over-ripeness, was only exacerbated by his perpetually red and perspiring face. And if all that were not enough, Bentley was prone to the most unnerving twitches – twitches that could vary in intensity from a mere tic or spasm to startling convulsions.

'I have informed Master Vyner of the situation regarding his schooling,' said Jerwood, backing away from Bentley a little. He tipped his hat to each of us. 'I have also informed him of his visit to Sir

Stephen. I shall bid you farewell. Until tomorrow, gentlemen.'

I felt a wave of misery wash over me as I stood there with the twitching Bentley. A child's fate is always in the hands of others; a child is always so very powerless. But how I envied those children whose fates were held in the loving grip of their parents and not, like mine, guided by the cold and joyless hands of lawyers.

'But see now,' said Bentley, twitching violently. 'There now. Dear me. All will be well. All will be well, you'll see.'

'But I don't want to go,' I said. 'Please, Mr Bentley, could I not spend Christmas with you?'

Bentley twitched and winced.

'Now see here, Michael,' he said. 'This is very hard. Very hard indeed.'

'Sir?' I said, a little concerned at his distress and what might be causing it.

'I'm afraid that much as Mrs Bentley and I would love to have you come and stay with us, we both feel that it is only right that you should accept Sir Stephen's invitation.'

'I see,' I said. I was embarrassed to find myself on the verge of tears again and I looked away so that Bentley might not see my troubled face.

'Now then,' he said, grabbing my arms with both hands and turning me back to face him. 'He is your guardian, Michael. You are the ward of a very wealthy man and your whole life depends upon him. Would you throw that away for one Christmas?'

'Would he?' I asked. 'Would he disown me because I stay with you and not him?'

'I would hope not,' he said. 'But you never know with the rich. I work with them all the time and, let me tell you, they are a rum lot. And if the rich are strange, then the landed gentry are stranger still. You never know what any of them will do . . .'

Bentley came to a halt here, realising he had strayed from the point.

'Go to Hawton Mere for Christmas,' he said quietly. 'That's my advice. That's free advice from a lawyer, Michael. It is as rare and as lovely as a phoenix.'

'No,' I said, refusing to change my grim mood. 'I will not.'

Bentley looked at the ground, rocked back and forth on his heels once or twice, then exhaled noisily.

'I have something for you, my boy. Your dear mother asked me to give this to you when the time came.'

With those words he pulled an envelope from his inside coat pocket and handed it to me. Without asking what it was, I opened it and read the enclosed letter.

Dear Michael,

You know that I have always hated taking anything from that man whose life your dear father saved so nobly at the expense of his own. But though each time I did receive his help it made me all the more aware of my husband's absence and it pained my heart – still I took it, Michael, because of you.

And now, because of you, I write this letter while I still have strength, because I know how proud you are. Michael, it is my wish – my dying wish – that you graciously accept all that Sir Stephen can offer you. Take his money and his opportunities and make something of yourself. Be everything you can. Do this for me, Michael.

As always and for ever,
Your loving mother

I folded the letter up and Bentley handed me a handkerchief for the tears that now filled my eyes. What argument could I have that could triumph against such a letter? It seemed I had no choice.

Bentley put his arm round me. 'There, there,' he said. 'All will be well, all will be well. Hawton Mere has a moat, they tell me. A moat! You shall be like a knight in a castle, eh? A knight!' And at this, he waved his finger about in flamboyant imitation of a sword. 'A moated manor house, eh? Yes, yes. All will be well.'

I dried my tears and exhaustion came over me. Resistance was futile and I had no energy left to pursue my objection.

'Come, my boy,' said Bentley quietly. 'Let us quit this place. The air of the graveyard is full of evil humours – toxic, you know, very toxic indeed. Why, I knew a man who dropped down dead as he walked away from a funeral – dead before he reached his carriage. Quite, quite dead.'

Bentley ushered me towards his carriage and we climbed inside. The carriage creaked forward, the wheels beginning their rumble. I looked out of the window and saw my mother's grave retreat from view, lost among the numberless throng of tombs and headstones.

CHAPTER TWO

I spent a restless night at the Bentleys' house in Highgate, packing to leave when I arose early the following day. As we journeyed to King's Cross station that afternoon I sat in silent contemplation of my many misfortunes. I felt resentful of all those – even, I am ashamed to say, my mother – who had conspired together to bring me to this state. Grief had swiftly given way to a deep and angry bitterness.

The sun was already sinking behind the new St Pancras Hotel when we arrived, and the difference between that tall and stylish edifice and the humbler, squatter King's Cross station reminded me a little of the difference between the two lawyers who now stood alongside me at the bustling station entrance.

My bag was unloaded and I seemed to be handed from the care of one lawyer into the care of the other with detached efficiency. I felt as though I were a bundle of legal papers rather than a person.

Having shaken Jerwood's hand, Bentley held his hand out to me and, when I took it, he placed the other on top so that my hand was all enclosed in his, and he smiled at me, twitching and blushing a little, glancing nervously at Mr Jerwood, as if kindness were some sort of misdemeanour among lawyers. Jerwood, for his part, looked in the direction of the large clock and remarked that it was really time we ought to be going.

'All will be well,' said Bentley quietly. 'All will be well.'

But I was not in the mood for kindness.

'Thank you for your services, Mr Bentley,' I said coldly.

I saw the look of hurt in his face and for a moment I felt a stab of guilt – but only for a moment. Mr Bentley smiled sadly, let go of my hand, tipped his hat and, saying farewell, walked away to be engulfed by the crowd.

'I rather think Mr Bentley may be a good man,' said Jerwood quietly as we watched him leave. 'I fear they're in short supply, so value them when you find them.'

I saw no cause to value anything about my present circumstances and I resented this lawyer for trying to influence me one way or another. I was perfectly aware that Mr and Mrs Bentley meant well, but I was tired of feeling beholden to people of whom I had asked nothing.

We entered the great station; I followed Jerwood, who strode with stately determination through the crowds. A locomotive belched out a plume of filthy smoke that sailed up towards the wide arch of the ceiling high above.

We found our platform and boarded our train, and had barely seated ourselves before it lurched out of the station with a squeal of wheel rims and a whistle of steam.

The journey to Ely was uneventful, and though I had travelled very little by railway and would normally have been much excited by such a trip, I sat in the carriage with the same dull disinterest as if I had been travelling by omnibus.

Jerwood was quite talkative in a dry and formal

way, though I gave him little encouragement. By and by I realised that his stiff manner was only a kind of awkwardness, and he seemed genuinely interested in me and in the answers I gave to his questions about my life. Much as it suited me to dislike him, I found myself warming to this stranger. In fact, it took all my willpower to maintain my sullen demeanour.

Though initially undeterred, Jerwood eventually took his lead from me and we settled into a state of quietude. The lawyer began to read through a mass of papers he had pulled from his briefcase. I wondered if any of them concerned my fate.

I looked out of the window, staring blankly at the passing view. Had the pyramids of old Egypt appeared on the horizon I should have paid little heed. I felt as though some part of me had died with my mother and that I would never again feel truly alive.

Exhaustion wrestled with misery for supremacy of my thoughts, but it was exhaustion – perhaps mercifully – which came out victorious, and I sank into a fitful sleep, lulled by the movement of the railway carriage.

My resting mind did not acknowledge the need for the barriers I had constructed while awake, barriers to those thoughts I found too upsetting to allow. Memories of my poor mother came to me uninvited, though once they came I would have done anything to be in their company for a lifetime and never to have woken up. Things hadn't been easy after my father died, but we were often happy, just the two of us. When wake I did, it was as if our parting was newly forced and the pain as fresh as ever. Tears stung my eyes as soon as they opened.

Only the desire not to appear weak and foolish in front of Jerwood dried my eyes. The lawyer was deep in the examination of the papers laid out on his lap and I looked out at the passing view.

'We will soon be in Ely,' said Jerwood, glancing up.

I made no reply. What did I care?

'A carriage will meet us at the station,' he continued, 'and take us on to Hawton Mere. It isn't too far.'

Again I made no reply. Jerwood shuffled his papers together and placed them on the seat beside him.

'Michael,' he said, 'I understand that you must feel the world is against you –'

'Do you, sir?' I said, turning towards him, my voice choking a little. How could a man like that understand what I felt?

'But you must realise that we are only trying to do what is best for you,' he continued.

'I don't want to go!' I said. 'I don't want to spend Christmas with people I don't know.'

Even as I said the words I realised that, with my mother gone, there could be no other kind of Christmas now. Better to spend it with the Bentleys, though. At least I knew them a little and knew them to be kindly. Jerwood nodded, as though reading these thoughts.

'I understand. It must be hard for you, I know,' he said. 'And I do sympathise, Michael. But give Sir Stephen a chance. He has made you his ward. It is not unreasonable for him to meet you, now, is it?'

I shrugged and looked out of the window again. It did not matter what I said. I was going to Hawton Mere whether I liked it or not. Jerwood gathered up his papers and began putting them away in his briefcase.

'About your guardian,' he said as he put the case down at his feet. 'I should warn you that Sir Stephen has not been well of late. I have known him for many years, ever since we were children in fact, and he is a good man, but he may not be quite what you expect.'

I had actually given very little thought to what

Sir Stephen may or may not have been like until that moment. Jerwood's words did nothing to improve my enthusiasm for meeting my guardian.

'Sir Stephen has the power to be a great force for good in your life, Michael,' said Jerwood. 'He made a promise to your father to help you and it is to his credit that he is honouring it.'

'My father died and he is alive,' I said. 'There's nothing he can do for me that will ever change that.'

Jerwood saw that further conversation on the matter was useless and turned to look out of the window, as did I. The day was ending, and the evening light gilded the steeples and the bare branches of high treetops. It sent long blue shadows across the rich brown earth of ploughed fields that were speckled with crows. The sky was clear and the cold air seemed to seep through the glass of the carriage as night approached. By the time we reached Ely the light of day was all but extinguished.

CHAPTER THREE

The ancient cathedral stood out against the dying light of evening, looking more like a formidable castle than a church. Its size and height were exaggerated by the fact that it sat atop a low hill that seemed a mountain in this flat fenland landscape, the great spiked tower bristling on the skyline like a giant's crown.

I waited next to my paltry luggage while Jerwood left in search of the carriage that would take us to Hawton Mere and my meeting with Sir Stephen. I suddenly felt chilled and weary and Jerwood must have seen this in my face when he returned.

'Come along,' he said quietly. 'Our carriage awaits.' Without another word, he set off, and I, fearing I would be lost in this strange place, picked up my bag as swiftly as I could and all but ran after him towards the carriage.

The driver was a tall, thin man and he was standing immediately below a gaslight so that the shadow from his hat darkened his face to a point just above his mouth, a mouth which seemed to curl into a sneer as I caught his eye. He stepped forward at our approach and tipped his hat to Jerwood, who nodded back, passing him first his own bag and then mine, before climbing into the carriage, with me close behind. I thought I heard the driver say something as I passed him; or rather I heard him make some kind of noise. But it could likewise have been the horse.

The driver whistled and flicked the reins and the carriage moved away, rattling through the town, its lanterns sending animated shadows leaping back and forth, and making the passing windows shimmer and flicker as though licked by the flames from some great fire.

Night was now in full spate and its inky waters had flooded the flatlands all about and they were black to the far horizon, where the sky was barely brighter than the land.

I had never been to these parts before, but knew that they had been marshes centuries ago, drained and transformed into black-soiled farmland. Looking from the carriage window was more like looking out from a boat across a wide uncharted sea, so untroubled was it by any sign of human habitation.

As on the train, I once more drifted on the edge of sleep. The rumble of the carriage wheels faded in and out of my consciousness: a sound like waves washing against shingle. I seemed to float on dark waters.

I dreamt I was standing among the headstones in Highgate cemetery, looking down at my mother's grave. Jerwood and Bentley were some yards away, whispering. Every now and again they would look towards me and laugh, their faces distorted and ugly.

I was aware of a movement among the shadows to my left and turned to see a figure – a small figure – running between the gravestones, hiding and then running again. It was always, always, in shadow and I could discern no features at all.

It scampered in a crazed and zigzag path, which I realised, with dread, was bringing it closer and closer to where I stood. When it came to the nearest headstone, it stayed hidden and did not re-emerge. I looked to Jerwood and Bentley but they now stood as still as statues, as if the whole world had come to a halt. I edged forward to look behind the headstone; a shadow leapt towards me with terrifying suddenness, smothering me in darkness, and I awoke with a start.

Jerwood nudged me and said that we should shortly be arriving at Hawton Mere and that if I looked I might catch my first glimpse of the house.

I leaned out of the carriage window, the combination of the cold night air and the rain that was now beginning to fall making me squint. But I could see nothing but a vague shape up ahead, blacker than the blackness beyond. Even so, I could tell that the structure was of some considerable size. A mist was combining with the drizzle to blur what little I could make out.

Just as I pulled my head back into the relative warmth of the carriage, the lanterns, whose glow did not extend much beyond the edge of the road, illuminated for a passing, startling moment a woman who loomed out of the night. Her arms reached out towards the carriage, her eyes wild and her face pale, her mouth wide with a cry that the rumbling wheels drowned out entirely. Despite the freezing temperature she appeared to be dressed in nothing but a linen shift and was soaking wet into the bargain.

'Sir!' I cried, turning to Jerwood. 'There's a woman, sir. By the road. I fear she may need some assistance.'

'A woman?' he said, springing forward and banging on the roof of the carriage with his cane. The driver immediately whistled to his horses and pulled on the reigns. The carriage came to a skidding halt and Jerwood and I both jumped out.

Jerwood grabbed one of the lanterns and we walked back down the road. There was a ditch running alongside and I was sure that the woman had stood just on the other side of it. But there was no sign of her.

We walked back and forth and peered into the gloom, lantern aloft, but there was nothing to see. On either side, the land fell away from the ridge along which the road ran: we might have been standing on a jetty surrounded by the sea.

I stared forlornly into the dark, unable to comprehend how she could have disappeared so completely. With her dress so white and the horizon so unbroken, it was hard to see how she could have hidden herself or run off in such a short space of time. And in any case, her face was one of urgent expectancy, of one desiring help or sympathy, not of one who planned to run away.

I turned from searching the darkness to find Jerwood standing in front of me, holding the lantern.

'Are you quite certain you saw her?' he asked.

'Yes, sir. Quite certain.'

'Well, I'm afraid there doesn't seem to be any sign of her now,' he said. 'Jarvis!'

The grim-faced driver had already climbed down and now walked towards us.

'Did you see anyone beside the road?' Jerwood asked.

Jarvis shook his head. The sleet was turning to snow and his black coat and hat were speckled with white. 'Not I, sir,' he said. 'I ain't seen a soul since we left Hawton village. Who'd be abroad on a night like this if they didn't have to be?'

Jarvis turned up his collar and spat into the gloom, giving me a look that made it plain that he thought I was a fool and Jerwood only a little better for humouring me.

'Hello!' I called out. 'Are you there?' But there was no response.

'Come,' said Jerwood, putting his hand on my shoulder. 'I think we should return to the carriage.'

I shrugged him away.

'But it's beginning to snow. She will surely catch her death if she stays out here tonight.'

'If we cannot see her, Michael, and she does not answer our calls, I'm not sure what more there is for us to do,' he said. 'You have been tired and dozing. Could you not have imagined it in the confusion between sleep and waking?'

'No, sir,' I said firmly.

'I'm sorry, Michael. There really is nothing more to be done.'

'But, sir,' I continued angrily, 'she was begging for our help. You can't just leave her!'

'Michael,' said Jerwood, a touch of irritation showing in his voice for the first time, 'if she wanted our help, why has she disappeared? Why beg for help and then hide when we stop?'

I took another look into the darkness, to the spot where I had seen the woman, and then turned back to Jerwood, who was already walking towards the carriage with Jarvis. I had no answer to his question and yet it seemed wrong to leave.

But though I felt angry and ashamed to do so, I could hardly stay and look for her myself with no light to aid me, and so I followed and climbed alongside him in the carriage.

We moved on and, seeing that Jerwood was neither going to look at me nor speak, I turned my attention to the window just as the carriage began to cross the bridge that spanned the moat. A single light glimmered in the blackness of the great walls of Hawton Mere, its golden glow reflected in the murky waters below. Then all at once it was gone, and we passed beneath the arch of the gatehouse and clattered out into the courtyard beyond.

CHAPTER FOUR

Jarvis jumped down and held the door open for us to leave the carriage. A manservant moved towards us, silhouetted against the lanterns that lit the courtyard.

'Mr Jerwood, sir,' he said, reaching for and taking the lawyer's bag. 'It's good to see you again. And this must be Master Vyner,' he added, looking at me. He was a thick-necked bull of a man, in his forties, about the same age as Jerwood. He wasn't tall but as powerfully built as anyone I had ever seen.

'Yes,' said Jerwood. 'Glad to see you too, Hodges.'

'There was a woman out on the road,' I

announced loudly. If I could not convince Jerwood to do something, then perhaps I could rouse some action from the servant.

'A woman?' said the servant, turning to Jerwood. 'Who was she, sir?'

'Master Michael thinks he saw someone in distress,' said Jerwood. 'But we stopped to look and could see no one there.'

'It could have been an owl, sir,' the servant suggested. 'You wouldn't be the first person who'd –'

'I did see someone!' I said.

The servant looked past me towards Jerwood. 'There is a gypsy camp nearby, sir. I can ask there in the morning if you like.'

'Thank you, Hodges,' said Jerwood. 'Will that satisfy you, Michael?'

'But she might be dead by then,' I said.

'I really think we ought –' Jerwood began.

'You don't believe me!' I said angrily. 'But she was there. I know she was.'

In truth I could not have said why I felt so agitated and so bold in my expression of that agitation. I suppose it was, as much as anything, a childish outrage at not being taken seriously by these adults. I knew what I had seen. Why could they not accept that?

I heard Jarvis snort as he led the horse away. Jerwood, the servant and I stood in awkward silence for a few moments, the gathering snow swirling around us. It was the servant who broke the spell.

'I can't send anyone out tonight, sir,' he said. 'The weather's closing in and you can't see your hand in front of your face out there. I'll go to the gypsies myself in the morning, but they don't take kindly to visitors after dark.'

I stood there in hot-blooded frustration, but I knew there was nothing I could do.

'My name is Hodges, Master Vyner,' continued the servant. 'Anything you need, you just ask for me. Let's get you out of this foul weather.'

With that he took my bag along with Jerwood's and set off. Jerwood followed, and after a moment I did the same, entering through a large door bristling with nails and coils of wrought iron.

As soon as I walked through that door I sensed it: a strange energy that filled the air and shone like a black light from every shadow. There was a whispering that rose and fell in volume – though I felt it rather than heard it. All my senses told me there was danger – deadly danger – and yet I saw nothing untoward, save for a grim and unwelcoming hallway.

'You are to stay with us over the festivities?' asked Hodges.

'Yes,' I said, while noticing how odd the word 'festivities' sounded in these surroundings. Could Hawton Mere ever be festive? It was hard to imagine.

Garlands of ivy were draped here and there and sprigs of glossy green holly glistened in vases and on windowsills in preparation for Christmas, but these decorative touches seemed only to draw attention to the grim nature of this place – like tying a ribbon to a gravestone. What kind of place was this?

My nightmare about the strange figure in the cemetery had no doubt unsettled my nerves, and those unsettled nerves had then been frayed further by the startling appearance of the woman on the road. But still I felt as though I had brushed against a strand of web and somewhere in the shadowy heart of that house a spider twitched. It was all I could do to stop myself from turning on my heels and running away. But where would I have run to?

'Michael?'

Jerwood was talking to me. Groggily I turned to face him.

'Are you all right?' he asked. 'You look pale.'

'I . . . I am . . .' I could not find the words to finish the sentence.

'You are fatigued after the journey,' Jerwood said.

'And hungry too, I shouldn't wonder,' Hodges added. 'Dinner will be served directly.'

The warmth and light and bustle of activity provided at least a welcome change from the cold and dark of the courtyard. But this contrast only served to remind me once again of the cruel fate of the woman on the road and the seeming heartlessness of those around me. Anger and frustration eventually seeped back in to wash away the sense of dread.

Mr Jerwood was clearly well known at the house. It was almost as if there was feeling of relief that he had come, as though he was a doctor rather than a lawyer. Not that I felt in any way that I was the beneficiary of any reflected affection. The servants, when they looked at me at all, did so with stolen, surreptitious glances.

'Sir Stephen and Miss Charlotte will be along presently,' said Hodges. 'Come into the kitchen, sirs, and warm yourselves.'

The kitchen was an enormous vaulted room, shining with copper pans and utensils of every kind, the walls heaving with plate racks. There was a huge cooking range at one end and an open fire alongside it. Hodges asked Jerwood if he would like a drink.

'I'll take a glass of brandy if you'll join me,' he replied.

'Aye, sir,' said Hodges. 'Let's sit by the fire a while.'

'Excuse me,' I said. 'But I need the . . . I need to . . .'

I was unsure of the correct term to be used in such a grand house, but Hodges took my meaning.

'There's a water closet across the hall, sir,' he said, pointing to the door through which we'd entered the kitchen. 'Just to the left of the staircase. Take a lamp with you.'

I left the two men alone. Hodges was setting down a bottle of brandy and two glasses on a table by the fire. I walked out into the vast entrance hall, struck by how dark it was in comparison to the kitchen. What illumination there was was provided entirely by candlelight and oil lamps that gave little light, and seemed only to increase the blackness of the shadows. I took it that the modern convenience of gas had not yet arrived at Hawton Mere.

A mighty soot-blackened fireplace stood on one side of the hall, its mantelpiece supported by two straining Amazonian females. On the other side, a great staircase rose up.

The floor was made of different shades of inlaid marble, set into a mosaic pattern that gave the unsettling illusion of being constructed of dozens of solid cubes. The effect was so convincing that I found myself wanting to hop from one to another, though the floor was quite flat.

To my surprise, the water closet contained a very modern flush lavatory, with a richly decorated bowl covered all over with a pattern of irises. It seemed so remarkably out of keeping with the ancient house and its dreary interior decorations.

But when I pulled the chain, the ancient plumbing groaned and vibrated and sounded as though it might explode at any moment. I could feel the tremors beneath my feet as I walked back towards the kitchen. Then something moved behind me.

I turned and, though I could see nothing there at all, I was sure that something was hidden in the shadow of the staircase. I went back to investigate.

There was a huge mirror there, with a gold frame. The frame gilt was missing here and there and the mirror pockmarked about the outer edges. It was rather like gazing into a frozen pool.

'I was terrified of that mirror as a child,' said a voice behind me.

I turned to see a tall, thin man. He was dressed all in black and was silhouetted against the candle-light. The effect was so strange that I stepped back, more than a little afraid. A huge wolfhound edged forward, head down, growling.

'Clarence,' said the man, as though to a child. 'Is that any way to greet a visitor?'

But, alarming though the wolfhound was, I saw very quickly that it was not me he was growling at, but the mirror behind me.

'I am your guardian, Michael,' said the man, holding out a hand. 'Sir Stephen Clarendon. I am very pleased to meet you.'

As he said these words he stepped into the light and I had my first glimpse of the man I had heard so much about and in whose hands my fate now rested.

He was pale and gaunt; his eyes were deep-set and peered out, twinkling dimly from beshadowed sockets. Long white hair was swept back from his high forehead and dripped into coils at his collar. He held out one of his long, pale hands for me to shake and I did not prolong the greeting: his hand was as cold as it looked. If there was a spider at the heart of this house, then surely it was he.

'Pleased to meet you, sir,' I replied without conviction.

'I was very sorry to hear about your mother,' said Sir Stephen.

'Thank you, sir.'

'You have your father's looks,' he said with a half-smile. 'Have you your father's courage, I wonder?'

'I don't know, sir,' I answered.

'Time will tell, eh?' he said. 'Time will no doubt tell. Your father was a good man and a very brave man, my boy. As you know, without him I would not be standing here today.'

I made no response and I think my expression betrayed my feelings that this seemed a poor trade. Sir Stephen narrowed his eyes a little and his smile flickered and died.

'This is my sister, Charlotte,' he said after a pause.

It was as if he had lit a lantern. As dark and gloomy as he was, so the woman that now stepped forward was like a bright flame.

'Michael,' she said, her dress swishing over the floor, and she embraced me as though I were a long-lost and dearly loved relative. 'I am very pleased to meet you.' Her voice was clear and pure.

Her skin, I distinctly remember, was like silk it was so smooth. She was pale too, but in her the paleness was like marble, finely carved, and framed by tumbling black ringlets. She was quite the most beautiful woman I had ever seen until that moment or since, and though her face was a little cool in its beauty, it changed its climate entirely when she smiled, as she did then.

'Pleased to meet you, ma'am,' I replied.

'*Charlotte*,' she corrected. 'We shall be friends, shall we not, Michael?'

'Ah, Sir Stephen,' said Jerwood, coming from the kitchen with Hodges. 'Good to see you again, sir. And Charlotte, you are looking as lovely as ever. You have met your ward, I see.'

'Tristan,' said Charlotte, 'you must tell me all the news from London over dinner. Perhaps you could show Michael to his room, Hodges?'

'Come along then, sir,' said Hodges, turning to me. 'I'll show you where you'll be sleeping.'

CHAPTER FIVE

Hodges fetched my bag from the hall and, picking up a lamp in the other hand, set off, with me in pursuit.

We climbed a wide staircase with carved wooden posts and a sweeping handrail smoothed by centuries of use. The walls of the stairwell were lined with a dark wallpaper covered all over with stylised foliage, so that every inch of wall space seemed to coil and sprout in a way that was quite dizzying to my eyes.

The light from the lantern created a bubble of relative brightness, like a white bloom shining in the midst of the dingy forest of foliage crowding in on us, and I clung to its glow with the dogged determination of a moth.

Grim portraits of Sir Stephen's ancestors stared out at me as I passed, their faces perched atop white lace ruffs like heads on dishes, looking at me with expressions that seemed to declare their disapproval of my presence in their house.

At the top of the stairs was a huge and rather sinister grandfather clock, bristling with carved pinnacles and curlicues, as ornate as a medieval bell tower and with a tick so deep and resonant that I could almost feel the teeth in my skull vibrate as I walked by.

I followed Hodges down a maze of corridors, hurrying to keep step with the servant, for I was all too aware of the darkness that moved like a great beast behind us. I had an unnerving sensation that it concealed something terrible, something I had a horror that I might see were I ever to turn my head. My heart had been fluttering ever since I arrived. I felt faint by the time we reached the door to my room.

I stepped in quickly after Hodges and he used his lamp to light another in the room. A fire was dying to red embers in the hearth, giving the place a welcome warmth of temperature and colour. But the effect was short-lived.

Just as a face betrays the life of the owner, so too a room carries a trace of the lives lived within its walls. This room positively ached with sadness. It was not just that the room was dark – and it was dark in furnishings and in its greedy accumulation of shadows – it was the very air that seemed tainted with misery.

I looked about me. A large bed with a carved wooden headboard came out from one wall and a washstand stood nearby. An ugly wardrobe with an oval mirror loomed in the shadows at the lamp-light's edge. When Hodges spoke, I gasped, startled, having forgotten he was there.

'There is a flushing lavatory at the end of the hall to the right,' said Hodges with a grimace. 'Miss Charlotte had them installed last year. But they are frightfully noisy devices, sir, as you may already have discovered. I would ask you to use the pot under your bed if you need to relieve yourself in the night.'

'Of course,' I said. 'Thank you, Mr Hodges.'

'Just Hodges, sir,' he said with a smile. 'Just call me Hodges.'

I nodded.

'Will that be all, sir?'

'Yes, I think so, Mr – sorry – Hodges.'

'Dinner will be served at eight, sir.' Hodges bowed a shallow bow and left the room, closing the door behind him.

I was thoroughly exhausted and I lost no time in getting changed while there was some remaining warmth from the fire. As I did so, I was startled to see a boy standing at the far side of the room.

I quickly realised that it was an illusion, however. It was a painting – a full-length portrait of a boy about my age, though of a much more slender build and very pale. It was the paleness and fine features of the face that put me in mind of Charlotte, and thence to Sir Stephen. I felt sure that I was looking at a portrait of my guardian as a boy, a theory that was confirmed by a label on the frame. There was a knock at the door and I turned to see Jerwood.

'Ah good, you are getting changed for dinner. I am just next door. When you are ready we can walk down together.'

'As you wish, sir,' I said. I confess I felt somewhat relieved.

Dinner was a rather strained affair. The dining room was large and the only illumination came from candlesticks on the tables, whose light barely reached the walls.

Sir Stephen sat at one end of the long table, Jerwood and myself on one side and Charlotte on the other. Charlotte did most of the talking, quizzing Jerwood continually about London society and the latest fashions, and it was clear that Jerwood knew or cared little about either.

When she had exhausted Jerwood's meagre knowledge of bonnets and dance steps, Charlotte turned her attentions to me and bombarded me with questions.

'Tell us about yourself, Michael,' she said. 'We know so little about you. What sort of interests do you have?'

'I . . . I don't know what to tell you,' I said.

'Well, let me see. Are you a boy who likes sport?' she asked. 'Are you a runner? You have the look of a runner about you, doesn't he, Stephen?'

I was too slow to reply and so Charlotte continued.

'Cricket, perhaps? All boys love cricket, I am told.'

'I like it well enough,' I replied.

When she saw there would be no further elaboration, she tapped her fingernails together with an audible patter and pursed her lips.

'Are you a scholar then?' she asked after a pause. 'Would you rather be in the library than on the sports field?'

I cast a quick glance at Jerwood, who I knew from our conversation in the cemetery had received a not very glowing account of my school life.

'I do enjoy reading,' I ventured.

'You do?' said Charlotte brightly. 'What sort of books do you like to read? History books? Myths and legends? Tales of adventure? *Novels?*'

She said this last word with a sour expression that betrayed her opinion of such works. I opened my mouth to reply, but Jerwood interrupted with what I firmly believe to be a wholly invented piece of gossip about a politician I had never heard of and so saved me from further inquisition.

Sir Stephen seemed content for others to dominate the conversation and said very little. My view of him was partially obscured by the flickering flame of a candle, but I just knew that he was studying me intently and I found this unseen gaze very discomfiting.

Then I became aware of Charlotte tapping her glass with her long fingernails as she listened to

Jerwood. *Tap, tap, tap. Tap, tap, tap.* But the noise began to change – to become a banging which seeped slowly into the fabric of the room. I lifted my head to try to determine the source, but it was clearly distant, even though the sound seemed to pulse through the walls. I watched as the water in my glass rippled in concentric rings. No one else appeared to take any notice.

Sir Stephen suddenly let out a groan and pushed himself away from the table.

'I rather think I may retire,' he said, getting to his feet and glancing at me with a look of wonder on his face.

'I'll come with you, Stephen,' said Charlotte, rising from her chair and exchanging a concerned look with Jerwood. Jerwood and I stood up too.

'Gentlemen,' she said, 'if you will excuse us.'

'Of course,' said Jerwood.

When they had left, Jerwood sighed and stared at the wine glass he cradled in his hand. I opened my mouth to speak, but he interrupted.

'Michael,' he said, 'Sir Stephen is suffering from a kind of nervous exhaustion. It grows ever more serious. I fear for his life, I really do. Every time I see him he seems so much frailer than before.'

I did not know what to say and so I said nothing.

'Come. We are all tired,' said Jerwood, getting to his feet. 'I think perhaps it would be best if we turned in.'

I followed Jerwood out of the dining room and up the stairs but we spoke not one word further until we bade each other goodnight in the passage-way outside Jerwood's room.

It was not until I was undressed and my head rested on the pillow that my thoughts returned to the woman on the road. I wondered where she was at that moment, picturing the terrible darkness that surrounded Hawton Mere.

The thought of that poor creature alone and unloved quickly mingled with my own sense of being friendless and trapped in this awful place, and this together with my sense of injustice at being dis-believed and disregarded soon brought tears. Alone in my room, I pulled my blankets round me, buried my face in the pillow and began to cry.

I tried to stifle the sound of my weeping, knowing that Jerwood was next door, but for a while despair overcame me completely and I curled myself up into a tight ball. So lost was I in my grief that it was some time before I registered that there was a strange echo to my sobs.

At first it seemed merely that they were amplified somehow and I thought this to be a product of the stillness and the disorientating blackness. But then I could hear that the sobbing was not quite in register with mine, as if two singers had begun to drift apart mid song. This effect was so odd that it gradually brought my sobbing to an end; but the echo continued. Someone else was crying – I was convinced of it.

In an instant I sobered up from the intoxication of my misery. Fear flooded in and my senses jumped to attention. The sobbing was still there, although it was becoming fainter as I listened intently.

I was about to get up from the bed – though I have to confess that the room was so dark I couldn't have been certain of which direction to walk in. But in any case, the sobbing had now ceased. The house was as silent as a monk.

I strained my ears to hear, but there was nothing save the panting breath issuing from my own dry lips. The glow from the fire seemed to expand as my eyes adjusted to the gloom and I became, by degrees, more sure that I was alone.

Then I remembered what Hodges had said about the water closet and recalled the extraordinary sound the plumbing had produced. I smiled to myself and eagerly embraced the notion that the noises I had heard were the hissing of water pipes.

All the same, the sound was so uncanny that I still felt the need to pull the blankets over my head so as to drown it out should it return, cursing whoever it was who had felt the need to use the lavatory.

CHAPTER SIX

The following morning I rose from my sleep a little uncertain as to where I was. The events of the previous day had become confused and dreamlike in my recollection. I struggled to make sense of what I had heard and seen. Above all, I was aware of feeling tense and apprehensive almost the instant I awoke.

I stood up dazedly and made my way to the window, pulling aside the heavy curtains. I hadn't looked out of the window before falling asleep and so had no idea whether my room faced the inner courtyard or, as I now realised it did, afforded a view across the wide expanse of fenland that surrounded this ancient house.

My window was somewhere near the gateway we had passed through in the night, and I could see now that the bridge that spanned the moat had two great stone creatures on either side – dragons or griffons or some such heraldic beast – whose twins also graced the balustrades on the stone steps up to the main door of the house.

Dank, impenetrable night had been replaced by a dazzlingly bright and ice-clear daylight, the sky almost white above. The light scattering of snow that had fallen in the night had frozen where it lay and the whole frosted land glinted as though dusted with sugar.

I could see the route Jerwood and I had travelled at night. The road – or more properly the track – was a long, straight and narrow causeway, with a ditch running alongside. I had an urge to leave the house that instant and march away. But where to?

What I had taken to be a heath, I now realised was in fact a bog: an endless mire full of hummocks capped with grasses and sedges, cow-parsley stalks and teasels, their leaves and seed heads rust-brown and black, shimmering here and there with the blue embers of a lingering frost. A flicker of light would gleam in this dead scene as the sky was reflected in the frozen ponds and creeks that filled the hollows and crevices of the marsh.

I was amazed at how far I was able to see. My view had been constrained to the point of blindness by the dark the night before, but the land was so flat and empty that it may as well have been obscured by a thick veil of mist for all the information the clarity afforded.

That said, there was something exhilarating about being able to see so far without any kind of interruption, either natural or man-made. For there was not a single other sign of human habitation for miles about and it was only at the far horizon that the scattering of spindly trees formed themselves into anything approaching a wood.

After a life spent in the confines of London, this gift of a view was both exciting and dizzying in equal measure. This house seemed horribly exposed, somehow, as if whatever ill winds might blow, there was only one place for them to strike: Hawton Mere.

This fearsome openness made my thoughts return to the distressed woman on the roadside. Seeing the bleak environment the house stood in made her predicament seem all the more awful and made me wonder at her eventual fate.

My memory of the woman had condensed and compressed itself into nothing more than the startling flash of her face in the lantern light and her desperate lunge out of the surrounding gloom as we sped past.

What had happened to bring her out in that state on such a night and why would she shun our assistance after appearing to beg for our help? Why would she hide? And, just as importantly, who was she?

As I was turning these thoughts over in my mind, there was a knock at the door and a maid came in. I blushed a little, standing there in only my nightshirt, but the maid seemed not at all concerned.

'Good morning, sir,' she said, putting a jug of hot water on the washstand and walking over to the fireplace. 'I hope you slept well.'

'Not too badly, thank you . . .' I said, waiting for her name.

'I'm Edith, sir,' she said.

Edith brought the fire back to life with practised ease and stood up, brushing the front of her dress. 'Breakfast is served in the dining room, sir,' she said before performing what I took to be a curtsey and leaving.

I washed and dressed and left my room and felt a little foolish when I realised that I was not at all sure of which way to go. I had been so tired the previous evening when Jerwood had accompanied me, and my foggy memory suggested only a maze of stairways and passages. I had no choice but to make my own way, and so I wandered off in what I felt must be the right direction.

As I was walking along a tunnel-like passageway, devoid of windows as it was and narrow, the thick walls billowing in and out, I heard a hammering noise, as if a door knocker was being rapped a long way off, as I had done at dinner the previous evening.

Two more steps and the sound grew in volume. That is to say, it grew in strength and power, for it was not that I heard it more clearly but that I felt it more strongly. It vibrated up from the floor and when I touched the wall it trembled rhythmically at the sound.

I found the effect disconcerting, and it added to the apprehensiveness I had felt since leaving my bedroom. I had the strongest sensation that I was being followed, a sensation not entirely allayed by my turning about every few steps to see if I might find somebody there. For although I never caught sight of a soul in those corridors, the act of looking only increased my sense that there was someone there, forever just out of sight.

Then there was a bang behind me. A door that I had just passed had been opened and slammed shut. When I retraced my steps the door was still vibrating on its hinges and the latch still rattling. The door was ajar and I pulled it open in time to hear the hammering noise clearer than ever. There was a short flight of steps leading down from the door and another, smaller, even darker, corridor curving away from the foot of them.

I peered in, but my curiosity was stifled by the feeling of anxiety that grew in intensity as I stood there. Then I heard another three bangs distinctly.

'Hello?' I called out.

There was no reply. The sound came again and I winced. It was as if it were inside my head. I moved through the doorway and walked down the steps. There was no one there, nothing to see.

The corridor I was now in didn't lead anywhere. I could make out an arched doorway at the far end, but it had been blocked up years – possibly centuries – before.

The darkness was encouraged and enriched by the wood panelling that lined the walls at either side. It was as high as my shoulder and as black as ebony. It was grim and gloomy, but no more so than anywhere else in the house, and yet once again I had that urge to run – to run and never stop until I was miles away from this place.

I was turning to go back up the steps when I heard another short volley of knocks. This time the sound seemed to be coming from beyond the panelling. I leaned forward and tapped a panel and it sounded with a distinctly hollow rap. The wall was evidently not solid behind it.

'Hello?' I called again.

There was no response but I felt sure that there was someone there – in whatever space lay beyond that panel. I had a growing dread of that place. The air in the passageway seemed fetid and poisoned and I was about to turn and get back to the main body of the house when something touched my shoulder and I cried out, leaping away. I turned to see Jerwood standing there.

'I didn't mean to startle you, Michael,' he said. 'Forgive me.'

I slid down the wall to sit on the stone floor and catch my breath.

'There's some kind of secret chamber behind that panel,' I said.

'Yes, there is. It's a priest hole,' he said, and seeing my look of confusion continued, 'It dates back to the sixteenth century and the reign of Queen Elizabeth. This was the house of a Catholic family and they hid Jesuits here – agents of the Pope in Rome. Those were harsh times. Capture would have meant bloody torture on the rack and a slow and gruesome execution.'

'It's a fearful place somehow,' I said, looking back at the panel.

'Yes,' said Jerwood. 'I rather think it is. How did you find it?'

'I heard banging, sir,' I said. 'It sounded like it was coming from inside.'

'Banging?' said Jerwood, frowning. 'But I was only yards away and I heard nothing at all. Besides, I don't think it could be coming from inside there –'

'Perhaps you think I'm a liar,' I said, standing up indignantly. 'But I'm not! I did hear banging and I did see that woman on the road!'

Jerwood crouched down and examined the panel.

'I apologise for offending you. I do not think you're a liar, Michael,' he said. 'But these panels were painted over years ago. Come and see. The paintwork is intact.'

Reluctantly, I shuffled over and looked to where Jerwood was pointing. What he said was absolutely true.

'Maybe there's another way in?' I suggested.

Jerwood shook his head.

'There is only this panel as entrance or exit,' he said. 'There isn't even a window. But I suppose it's possible that a mouse or rat has found its way in there . . .'

'But I heard banging, sir,' I said. 'I promise you. It couldn't have been an animal. I don't understand why you couldn't hear it, but I didn't imagine it. I swear.'

I was less confident than I tried to sound on this score. There was something strange about the way I heard the noise. I felt as though I had become trapped in a place between dreams and real life, the one merging with the other. Jerwood smiled and patted my arm.

'Calm yourself, Michael,' he said. 'I believe you.'

'You do?' I said, a little relieved to hear it.

'That is to say, I believe that you heard *something*,' said Jerwood. 'But didn't Hodges say something about the plumbing? Could it not have been the pipes banging?'

I opened my mouth to argue, but Jerwood held up a finger.

'Could it not at least be *possible* that the noise was made by the plumbing?'

I had to concede – reluctantly – that it was possible.

'This place has a particular significance to Sir Stephen and I don't think it would be wise to mention these noises to him,' said Jerwood. 'When I have more time, I may tell you about it. He may tell you himself when he knows you better. But you can see how fragile his nerves are.'

'What is the matter with him?' I asked.

Jerwood took a deep breath.

'Sir Stephen has been a troubled soul for much of his life, ' he said. 'But his late wife made him as happy as I think he is capable of being. Her death was a heavy blow to him. Grief can harm the best of minds, Michael.'

Here he looked at me and reached out to lay a hand tenderly on my shoulder.

'I would ask you to do me the favour of not mentioning this,' he said. 'I have my reasons, believe me, and I will tell you them at some later date. But for now I would simply ask that you say nothing about the priest hole. Can I rely on you?'

I was taken aback and more than a little moved by Jerwood's friendly tone, and, after a moment, I nodded my assent. In any event, like a dream, the noise and the hearing of it was already becoming so vague in my mind that I could no longer cling to it with any surety.

'Good man,' said Jerwood. 'Come – let's go to breakfast.'

CHAPTER SEVEN

I ate breakfast with little enthusiasm. I had never wanted to come to this place at all and now that I was here I could think of nothing but escape. I felt as though I had walked into a fog of mystery and whispers.

I wondered about the strange banging I'd heard and what Jerwood could mean about the priest hole having 'special significance'. Could it really be the plumbing? I couldn't get the image of the woman on the road out of my head either. There was definitely something going on here. I could feel it in every fibre of my being. Jerwood was keeping something to himself. But what? Any immediate possibility of finding out was quickly extinguished.

'Michael,' said Jerwood, sitting back in his chair. We were alone in the dining room. 'I have to leave Hawton Mere this afternoon for a few days. There is some urgent business in London I must attend to.'

'You're leaving me here on my own?' I said, dropping my knife with a loud clatter on to the plate.

Jerwood smiled and raised his eyebrows.

'I'm touched that you will miss me,' he said. 'I had thought that you might be glad to see me gone.'

I smiled at this myself. Before that moment I would have thought the same, but, friendless as I was, Jerwood was my one link to the world outside of this dreary place and the one person with whom I felt, in some small degree, comfortable.

'Will you come with me for a walk before I go?' he asked.

'Why, sir?' I asked. 'Where?'

'Well, I thought we might have a look around at the place you saw the woman last night,' he said.

I took note of the fact that Jerwood did not say 'thought you saw', and smiled.

'Besides,' he continued, 'it will do you good to get some fresh air.'

It was hard to disagree with that, and so I put on a coat and followed Jerwood, who had done likewise, out of the door and into the chill of the courtyard. The air was so cold that it hit my face like a slap, but it was certainly invigorating.

We walked under the arch of the gatehouse, Clarence barking at us from the courtyard as we passed, and out on to the bridge that was the only route off the little island upon which the old house stood.

Turning, I saw Hawton Mere standing like a castle, dominating the land all about it. The mighty walls were here and there punctured by windows and topped by tiled roofs. A tower rose up, crowned with a small pyramidal spire which was tiled like the roofs, and a golden weather vane sparkled in the sunlight. Great chimneys stood along the roof ridge like sentinels, smoke pluming from their heads. Part of me held out a feeble hope that we were going to keep on walking away from Hawton Mere and not stop until we got to Ely and the train to London. But after about half a mile, Jerwood came to a halt.

'Look,' he said, clapping his hands together. 'What do you think?'

'About what, sir?' I asked.

He raised his arm theatrically and pointed to a scarecrow standing beside the road in a patch of sugar beet. I looked at the scarecrow and then back to Jerwood, a little baffled.

'Come now,' said Jerwood. 'Look again. It was dark, the sleet was in your eyes, you were exhausted . . .'

'No, sir,' I said, seeing his meaning. 'I didn't see a scarecrow sir. I didn't see an owl either. It was a woman. She moved. She was calling out. Her face is as clear to me as yours, sir.'

Jerwood rested his hand on my shoulder.

'And there really is no possibility that you could have been mistaken, Michael? None at all?'

'No, sir,' I said. 'I know what I saw. Why will you not believe me?'

'It's not a question of believing or not believing –'

'But it is, sir!' I said vehemently. 'That's just what it is. If you told me, I would believe you.'

'Yes, Michael,' said Jerwood with a smile. 'I think perhaps you would.' He shrugged his shoulders and shivered. 'I'm a lawyer. I look to the evidence. I simply cannot understand why someone would ask for our help and then disappear when we stopped to give her the assistance she craved. It makes no sense.'

'I know, ' I said. 'I've gone over it in my head a

dozen times. But whether it makes sense or not, that's what happened.'

I looked back towards Hawton Mere. Even from this distance it seemed malevolent: a monstrous toad waiting to pounce.

'Besides,' I said, waving my arm at the scarecrow, 'this is nothing like what she was wearing. I only caught a glimpse of her, but even so, I could tell that she was just dressed in some thin linen shift; that was all.'

Jerwood had been pacing around, but at these words he stopped in his tracks and turned to me. The look on his face was a little like the expression Sir Stephen had worn in the dining room just before he left us. It was a look of wonderment.

'What did you say?' he asked.

'I said that she was wearing nothing but a linen shift, sir.' I was a little concerned by his sudden change of tone. 'She was soaked to the skin, her hair coal-black, all wet and dripping. She was pale, sir: deathly pale.'

Jerwood turned away, holding his head in his hands and muttering. He gazed back towards Hawton Mere. When he looked back at me, his expression was a mixture of confusion and sadness.

'Why did you not say this at the time?' he asked.

'I tried to,' I said. 'But no one was listening to me.'

Jerwood glanced this way and that, as though he thought the woman might suddenly appear. A flock of birds flew by, their wings whistling as they passed.

'Do you know who she is?' I asked.

He looked at me for a long time, his face flickering with thought.

'No,' he said after a long pause, shaking his head and walking swiftly away. 'No, I don't,' I heard him say again, as if to himself. But everything in his expression said that he did.

I did not see Jerwood again until lunch, and with Charlotte there I did not feel able to broach the subject. No sooner had we finished eating than the lawyer was readying himself to leave.

I walked out on to the road to see his carriage off and as it drove away up the track and away from Hawton Mere, I heartily wished that I was sitting alongside Jerwood. He looked at me and waved and his face bore the same curious expression as on the road that morning. What did he know and why would he not say?

I carried on up the track as far as the scarecrow. Its ragged dress fluttered in the breeze. Its crudely drawn face stared back at me from its sacking head and I turned away, back towards the house. How stark it looked. How bleak. All human life was hidden from view. Hawton Mere seemed to close in on itself, wrapping its heavy walls all about like a great cloak. I trudged back to the house with a heavy heart but resolved to at least attempt what Jerwood had asked: to accept that this was an ordeal that had to be undergone for the sake of my future freedom. All I had to do was see out the next few days.

CHAPTER EIGHT

As unlikely as the notion of missing Jerwood may have seemed a day or two before, all the misgivings I had harboured about staying in that house multiplied at his departure. For one thing, dinner without Jerwood was even more awkward, if such a thing were possible. Sir Stephen was still feeling unwell and so Charlotte and I were left alone. But it was as if the lawyer was the only common ground we had and without him we were lost for words.

Charlotte had apparently exhausted her supply of questions the previous evening and struggled to make any conversation at all. To be fair, she received precious little assistance from me in that regard. We ate the vast majority of the meal in silence.

That night, to my surprise, I slept soundly and woke refreshed. Sunlight streamed in through my bedroom window and some of my inner gloom seemed dispelled by its touch.

As I dressed I looked at the portrait of the young Sir Stephen, bathed now in light, and saw clearly for the first time what a strange and dismal figure he was even then, his expression part-way between sadness and fear.

I wondered to myself if a person could be born with a melancholy disposition, or had something happened to him some time before this picture was painted? Or maybe, I thought, it was simply this house. Too long a time spent in such a joyless place was bound to take its toll on a young mind. All the more reason, I reminded myself, to leave Hawton Mere as soon as I could.

Charlotte joined me for breakfast. Our conversation was no less stilted than it had been the previous evening, but she did seem in better spirits. She encouraged me to roam where I wanted in the house, so long as I did not disturb Sir Stephen by going to his study in the tower. I had no desire whatsoever to do that, so it was hardly an issue.

'Come along, I want to show you something,' said Charlotte when we had finished. With that she linked her arm through mine and led me through the hall and then a number of rooms until she opened one of two very tall doors to reveal an enormous library.

'This is my favourite room in the house, Michael,' said Charlotte. 'I have loved it ever since I was a little girl.'

As we moved through the room, she brushed the shelves and the books they held with her hand, gently, as though they were the flanks of beloved horses.

'My father was not one for great shows of affection,' she said, 'but he did indulge my mother's love of books. It was she who built up this library. It is her memorial.'

Charlotte turned to me and smiled, sensitive perhaps to the effect this talk of her mother might have on me, but it did not make me sad. If anything it lightened my heart to think that we shared some fellow feeling on this subject.

'I will leave you now, Michael,' she said. 'Enjoy the books.'

I was touched that Charlotte trusted me to be

left alone in the library among those treasured books and, eager not to lose that trust, I stood a while in awe of the place, not quite daring to actually handle any of its works.

The library contained more books than I think I had ever seen in one place. I had discovered my enjoyment of reading during my mother's illness. Before that I had never really understood the appeal – or indeed the purpose – of reading for pleasure, but I now found that I could spend hours with no other diversion than the solitary exercise of reading a book, and by the vehicle of those pages would be transported to faraway lands on fantastic adventures. More and more this love of reading had become a medicine and tonic for my troubled heart and mind.

But the library at Hawton Mere made few concessions to the interests of children. I did spend some time looking through a beautifully illustrated book about birds, but I soon tired of atlases and encyclopaedias and left the library in search of something else to keep me amused.

Hawton Mere was an ancient house and so did not have the layout of a normal dwelling. The rooms followed on one from another in a vast wheel, each room much as the last, filled with great gloomy beasts of furniture. Some squatted in corners, some reared up against dark wood panelling and walls papered in dizzying patterns of deepest red and green and blue.

Dour faces stared down at me from filigreed picture frames, and trophy stag heads fixed me with their dead eyes. Stuffed birds perched warily under dusty glass domes.

The more I walked the circuit of the house, the more uneasy I became. I began to have a sensation of walking a maze, turning corner after corner, not knowing what it was I was going to find at each turn. Then, returning to the hall, I found Clarence the wolfhound standing in front of me and my heart skipped a beat.

'Don't mind Clarence,' said Hodges, walking in through the door with a basket of logs. 'He won't hurt you. Go and say hello to Master Michael, you silly dog.'

With that, Clarence loped forward and nudged my hand until I stroked his head. The great beast's tail began to wag and I looked up to see Hodges with a grin on his face.

'He likes you, sir,' he said.

'Does he?' I asked.

'Oh yes,' said Hodges. 'Bit the hand off the last

boy who tried to stroke him.'

Hodges laughed at the look of horror that must have appeared on my face.

'I'm only joking, sir,' he said with a chuckle. 'Clarence wouldn't hurt a fly.'

I wasn't entirely convinced of Clarence's gentle nature, but I was sure he meant me no harm. He was evidently not allowed beyond the hall, however, because he stopped at the door as I continued my travels, whimpering a little at being left behind, until Hodges called him into the courtyard.

I continued my explorations. The house now seemed deserted and a curious expectant hush had descended, like that in the moment before a clap of thunder. From every wall and every mantelpiece a clock was ticking, and this ticking deepened and synchronised until it became the hammering I had heard before. Every reflective surface in the house appeared to tremble at its beat. How could I be the only one who heard it?

I moved from room to room, retracing my steps in a circuit of the house, searching for the source. Once again I stood at the top of the stairs leading down to the priest hole.

I had not appreciated it before, but the stone steps led down into the walls themselves, creating a passageway bored into a hidden place beneath the skin of the house.

I was determined to know what was making that noise and that determination was enough to overcome my sense of unease and allow my feet to move down the steps.

The banging was definitely louder now and there could be no doubt about it. Someone was inside that place. Whatever Jerwood said about there being no other entrance, someone was banging on the inside of that panel, desperately trying to get out.

I rushed to the panel and pushed, but it wouldn't move. I searched for some kind of lock, but there didn't seem to be one. I pushed again and this time the panel opened inwards with such sudden ease that I tumbled forward.

There was actually quite a drop and the shock of falling in and the pain of landing, combined with the impenetrable darkness, utterly disorientated me.

Then something moved. I didn't see it, as the feeble light coming in from the open panel illuminated nothing.

'Hello?' I said, my voice sounding frail and feeble. 'Is there someone there?'

All at once I knew that I had to get out of that place. Whatever it was in there with me, it was not right; it was not right at all. I could sense it readying itself to move, to pounce.

I turned and sprang for the open panel, but the thing in there was quicker. I felt – no, sensed – it brush past me at speed, hurling itself at the hole. I saw a shadow pass in front of me and the panel door was slammed shut.

Blackness. Utter blackness. I leapt at the place where the light had been, clawing at the panel with my fingernails, but it seemed sealed shut once more. I was trapped!

The panel would not budge. I banged and shouted, but there was no response. I listened, my ear pressed against the wood, but the only sound was my own gasping breath. I banged again and called out. The blackness was so thick it felt as though I were breathing it in and choking on it. I felt as though I were drowning in ink.

I pounded on the back of the door until my fist hurt, and I began to wonder if all noise was so effectively smothered by those thick walls that no one would ever hear the blows, just as no one was going to hear the oaths and curses I bellowed.

I slumped down, drained by my exertions at the

door. I was in no danger, I told myself. Surely I would be missed before too long and, though it was a big house, there were only so many places I could be. I must not panic.

But however calmly I talked to myself, that place was too foul to allow such efforts to slow my galloping heartbeat. With my sight denied by darkness, all my other senses seemed honed to a new sharpness. Something reached out towards me, I was sure of it – so sure I raised my arm to fend it off, but of course felt nothing there.

But feeling nothing did not soothe my spirits. No sooner had I lowered my arm than I was just as convinced that something was crawling towards me. I kicked out with my feet; again, I felt only the dank air about me.

These were phantasms of the mind, I told myself, nothing more, nothing more. They could not hurt me. They were not real. And yet with every passing second I became surer that there was more than my mere imagination at work in that place. There was something there. Something vile and terrible: a darkness made physical.

I hammered at the panel again, my blows becoming both more desperate and more exhausting. I could not even see my own fists pounding in front of my face, but they throbbed with pain. A deeper blackness within that foul gloom was congealing at my back, its cold and terrible presence chilling my blood. At any moment I felt that it would overwhelm me and smother me in its pitiless embrace. I yelled out with all the force my choking lungs could muster.

Suddenly the panel opened. Light from the passageway that had once seemed so dull and feeble now shone in like a dazzling sunburst.

I scrabbled out as if I had the hounds of hell biting at my feet and leapt across to the other side of the passageway, my whole body shaking with fear. Big arms enfolded me and a kindly voice comforted me. It was Hodges.

'Master Michael,' he said. 'What on earth were you doing in there, sir?'

I tried to reply, but my mouth was unable to shape the words. I looked up and was startled to see a figure standing in the doorway at the top of the steps who, to my slowly adjusting eyes, was little more than a silhouette. As I blinked and tried to make out who he was, he shrank back, covering his face, pressing himself into the wall, whimpering, looking from me to the priest hole and then back to me. To my astonishment he began to scream.

Hodges left my side and moved towards him as Charlotte swept into view, her face pale and confused as she tried to understand what was happening. It was only when she embraced the screaming figure that I realised it was Sir Stephen.

I began to try to speak but the sound of my voice seemed only to intensify his mania and he renewed his terrible shrieking with increased vigour, shielding his face with his arms, staring out between them like a madman. Hodges bade me be still and Charlotte took Sir Stephen away.

'Take Michael to the morning room and wait for me there,' she said as she left.

'Yes, ma'am,' said Hodges.

I took one last look at my terrified guardian, whose face I could just make out over Charlotte's shoulder, and then followed Hodges. The screaming rang out along the passageway, following me along, but by the time I reached the staircase it had calmed.

I stood in the morning room with Hodges, not knowing what to do. The door to the hall was open. Other servants went to and fro about their business, glancing at me as they did so, looking up at the stairs and in the direction of the earlier screams. A large portrait hung above the fireplace showing a stout, square-jawed man. He scowled down at us, as though ready to box our ears for the impertinence of looking at him.

'Sir Stephen's father,' said Hodges, following my gaze.

I marvelled at how different he was from his children. They had clearly inherited their fine features and delicate frames from their mother. I could see nothing of this brutish man in them at all. Within a few moments Charlotte came down.

'What were you doing there?' she said quietly as she entered the room, closing the door behind her.

'I meant no harm,' I said. 'I heard . . .' But I remembered what Jerwood had said and thought better of saying what I had heard. 'I was exploring the house, ma'am.'

She smiled and half closed her brilliant blue eyes.

'Charlotte,' she corrected. 'Sir Stephen is not well, Michael.'

'I'm sorry if –'

She held a finger to her lips to signal silence.

'You were not to know,' she said. 'You are a child and children are inquisitive and irresponsible.'

She said these words without a trace of admonishment. She smiled sweetly as if she were merely stating the obvious, and I could think of naught to do but nod at my own inquisitiveness and irresponsibility.

'I can see that you are shocked at my brother's appearance, but Sir Stephen's health is precarious. Please do not think badly of him, but please understand that he must not be excited in that way.'

'I'm sorry,' I repeated, unable to think of anything else to say.

'I know you are,' said Charlotte kindly. 'It must be very difficult for you. You have been through so much yourself of late. But I must get back to Sir Stephen. He will sleep now, but he will want me to be there when he wakes. We will talk later, Michael.'

Charlotte turned and swished away, her dress slithering across the marble floor. I watched her climb the stairs and then turned to Hodges standing beside me.

'Come along, Master Michael,' he said, patting me on the arm. 'Come and sit with me in the kitchen for a bit, eh? Mr Jerwood asked me to take special care of you while he was away and that's what I intend to do.'

CHAPTER NINE

I followed Hodges into the kitchen, the hot air hitting us in the face as we walked through the door. The kitchen was a different world compared to the chilly gloom of the rest of Hawton Mere: the fire glowed like a setting sun and painted every surface with its golden light.

Servants shared jokes and sang and whistled as they worked. They had created a sanctuary here and I fancied that if I could stay there for the whole of my sojourn at Hawton Mere, then things would not be so very bad. But I knew, just as Hodges knew, that Sir Stephen and Charlotte would never permit such a thing. I was to be a gentleman now. I could not be allowed to live among servants.

Besides, the servants were too busy to spend time with me. For all his promise to pay special attention to me, Hodges had his duties to perform, which were many and allowed him little time to sit and keep me company. In no time at all I felt as though I was simply in the way and left the kitchen unnoticed.

It was not until I crossed the bridge and left the confines of the shadowy courtyard that I felt the welcome heat of sunlight on my face. But sunshine did not lift the mood of Hawton Mere or the marsh that spread about it. The effect of those great, thick, high walls was still one of overwhelming gravity and gloom, but I found that at least by daylight – and from the outside – it held no special dread for me.

The sun shone out of a pale and dazzling blue sky and I had to squint into the brightness of the day, my eyes having become too accustomed to the dinginess of the house. The frosted marshes twinkled as though scattered with diamonds and sapphires. For the first time I was awake to the possibility that this landscape could be thought beautiful.

The air was clear and the horizon line was as sharply focused as the edge of the moat. I could see for miles. And this seeing for miles gave me the curious sensation of being on show. For though I was alone, the fact that I seemed to be the only living thing out in the open made me feel like a specimen on a dish.

Just as I thought this, I sensed something rushing towards me through the marsh. I heard a whispering gathering strength behind me, but when I turned there was nothing there. Again the whispering at my back, as if something were running towards me through long grass, but again on turning round I saw nothing. Nothing.

I stood in silent bafflement. And the silence was now absolute and just as disturbing in its way as the whispering had been, for it was as though I had become deaf in that instant.

Then I saw movement from the corner of my eye. Blurred movement. White. Something white moving by the house. It flew – no, *fell*. I turned and whatever it was had gone, although the echo of it was still there in my mind's eye, clinging like a dream on waking.

I ran in that direction. It was the area of the moat under a lichen-covered stone balcony. Had something fallen from that balcony? Had someone fallen into the moat? I skidded to a halt, staring at the ice.

There was nothing there. Nothing troubled the frozen surface, nor had anything fallen through: the ice lay unbroken all about. Neither had there been a sound of any kind.

Could Jerwood be right after all? Could I really have imagined the woman that night? Grief can damage a mind, he had said. Had grief damaged mine? I suddenly felt less sure of things.

I wandered back to the house in something of a daze. I was about to climb the stairs to investigate which of the upstairs rooms it was that had that balcony when Sir Stephen emerged from the shadows. He must have been standing in front of the mirror he said had held so much terror for him as a child. By the expression on his face, it was not without its terrors now.

'Michael,' he said.

His face seemed thinner, if such a thing were possible, his body tense, as though waiting for an explosion. The memory of him screaming like a madman came back and I flinched from him.

'Sir?' I answered.

'I wanted to talk to you about this morning,' he said.

'I'm sorry, sir.' I paused on the steps. His whole body seemed arched towards me as if he were about to pounce. I could not help but back away. 'I had not meant to ... I only heard a noise and ...'

He strode over to me so swiftly that I involuntarily recoiled, tripping over in the process.

'You heard a noise?' he said. 'A noise? What noise?'

Each repetition of these words was spoken at increasing volume as he loomed over me, his pale, skeletal fingers clutching at the air between us.

'Stephen!' called a voice behind him. It was Charlotte.

Sir Stephen did not move at first. I had assumed he was angry with me, for some unexplained reason, but his expression was not one of anger. Rather it was one of crazed inquisitiveness. He continued to look at me, his face only inches from mine, searching – or appearing to search – for something. But what?

'Stephen,' said Charlotte again, 'you are frightening your guest. I think we have all had a little too much excitement for one day.'

Sir Stephen blinked, his eyes losing their manic sparkle by degrees. His fingers flexed in front of my face and he stepped back, putting his hand to his temple and straightening himself. I stayed pinned against the panelling on the staircase, happy to keep as much distance between us as possible. Clarence trotted up the stairs to stand beside me, looking at Sir Stephen warily as though he did not know him.

'I . . . I . . . must apologise, Michael,' said Sir Stephen, without looking at me. 'Forgive me.'

With that he turned and climbed the stairs, slowly at first, but with a gradually quickening step until by the top step he was almost running. Within seconds he was gone.

I wondered how unhinged my guardian's mind might be. I was still a little shaken. The way he loomed over me on the stairs – I could believe him to be dangerous. I looked to Charlotte, who was still gazing up towards the top of the stairs. She took a weary breath and then turned to face me. I thought she would be angry that I again seemed to have been the unwitting cause of one of Sir Stephen's nervous attacks, but I was wrong.

'Come along, Michael,' she said, holding out her hand. 'I know for a fact that Mrs Guston has a large piece of pie left over. You will never taste a better apple pie in all England, I promise you.'

We walked those few steps, Charlotte's arm

through mine as if we were old friends, and by the time we reached the warmth of the kitchen I was once more at my ease.

'I'm afraid I have things I must attend to,' said Charlotte. With that she leaned forward and kissed me on the cheek, which blushed instantly at the touch of her lips.

She smiled at my embarrassment and, without saying another word, turned and walked away, her dress whispering quietly against the floor tiles, like children in a church.

Mrs Guston's apple pie was every bit as excellent as Charlotte had promised and I confirmed that to the cook herself, who stood over me, hands on hips, while I ate. She turned out to be a very friendly woman indeed, fussing about me and clapping her hands together every now and then, causing small explosions of flour.

'It's lovely to have a young lad in the house again, Master Michael,' she said. 'There hasn't been a child in the house since Sir Stephen and Charlotte were youngsters. And me and Hodges along with them.'

'You have been in the house since you were a child as well, Mrs Guston?' I asked, taking a swig of milk.

'Well, since I was about your age,' she said. 'My

mother was cook then, and I worked in the kitchen. Mr Hodges was a pageboy for Sir Stephen's father. There's a painting of him in the morning room.'

'Yes,' I said. 'I've seen it.'

Mrs Guston's tone had changed as she'd mentioned Sir Stephen's father and her expression soured. It was plain that she hadn't been at all fond of him and Mrs Guston did not strike me as a person who disliked people without reason. I had the same impression from Hodges. I wondered if the grimness of the house was his legacy.

'We had some happy times back then,' said Mrs Guston. 'We still do on this side of that door.' She nodded to the kitchen door. 'But the house has become a sad old place, Michael. It needs children. A house needs children.'

'Did Sir Stephen and Lady Clarendon not want children?' I asked.

'Oh, Lady Margaret was desperate for a child, God rest her soul,' said Mrs Guston. 'It's just a pity that you couldn't have come here when she was alive. Oh, it was a different place then, Master Michael.'

She had her back to me at this point but I saw her lift a cloth to her eyes and her voice was breaking as she spoke.

'There's not a day goes by when I don't think of her,' she said. 'She was the kindest person you could ever meet. But she was too good for this house.'

'What do you mean?' I said.

Mrs Guston turned and I saw the tears twinkling in her eyes.

'Don't mind me,' she said. 'I'm a silly old thing.' But then her face became serious. Her rosy cheeks seemed suddenly to dim. 'Nothing will make me understand how she could do it.'

'Do what, Mrs Guston?' I said.

'How she could –'

'Mrs Guston,' said Charlotte, coming into the kitchen. Mrs Guston jumped to attention, dropping the cloth and busying herself. 'Could you make a pot of tea for Sir Stephen?'

'Of course, ma'am,' she said.

'Is everything all right?' Charlotte asked, looking from the cook to me and then back again.

'Oh, quite all right, ma'am,' said the cook. 'I was chopping onions, is all.'

Charlotte smiled and left. Mrs Guston took a deep breath and smiled at me.

'Never mind me, sir,' she said. 'I'm just a silly old so-and-so. You run along now, Master Michael.'

CHAPTER TEN

Sir Stephen did not join Charlotte and me for dinner that evening, but he certainly made an appearance in my dreams that night, looming out of shadows and scuttling up darkened stairways like a hideous insect.

It was starting to feel as though some monstrous joke was being played on me: to have the benefit of a wealthy benefactor, but to find that benefactor seemingly a step away from the madhouse. What good was a guardian who was so deranged? What crazy purpose did he have for me at that house and how long must I wait to discover it?

I breakfasted alone the following morning. Clarence waited for me in the hall now, expecting to be patted before I went into the dining room. I was happy to oblige.

I returned to my room and spent the next few hours leafing through some books I had brought there from the library. I was particularly taken with a book by the famous artist and travel writer Arthur Weybridge, about his adventures in Asia Minor. It was dedicated to his son, Francis, who had died in tragic circumstances on the expedition.

But Francis's fate notwithstanding, I was enchanted with the wonderful drawings of those exotic locations and the descriptions of what he found there. The Turkish heat seemed to shimmer before my eyes. What a contrast with cold, damp Hawton Mere. It made me yearn to travel.

Eventually I made my way towards the dining room for lunch, hurrying past the door that led to Sir Stephen's tower. As I did so, it occurred to me that, since the tower had loomed above it, I must be near the room that led on to the stone balcony from which I had seen something fall the day before.

Sure enough there was a doorway not far from where I stood, which must, I reasoned, be the one, but when I tried the door I found it locked. I gave up and carried on my way.

At the top of the stairs that took me down to the hall, I paused to look at the curious grandfather clock with its image of a smiling sun above the left side of the face, and of a sad-looking moon and stars on the right. The moon reminded me a little of Hodges and I smiled to myself at the thought.

I was standing admiring it when I heard a noise below and walked down the stairs thinking I might find Clarence the wolfhound. But when I got there, I could see nothing but my reflection in the big old mirror that lived in the perpetual shade of the staircase. I was about to walk on when I saw a shape move in the glass behind me.

I turned but there was no one there. I stepped round the staircase to check the hall, but it was deserted. I went back to the mirror and looked at it once more. To my amazement, the shadowy figure was there again. It was clearer now, although still dark and still stretching and twisting. Distorted or not, as I approached the glass I could tell the shape was that of a boy, though utterly malevolent and pent up with a kind of poorly suppressed rage that almost bent his body in two and turned his hands to claws.

One moment it appeared as no more than a

shadowy boy, the next it was barely human. No matter how hard I tried to focus on its features, the shadowed reflection was forever blurred and indistinct, as if it were liquid constantly on the verge of dissolving into the blackness around it.

Suddenly the reflected boy-creature lurched forward and my heart skipped a beat. The glass bent and bubbled, flexed and juddered, as though it could not bear the task of mirroring that thing, and before I could step away, with a great crack it shattered as if struck by a hammer.

The noise brought Hodges running from the courtyard and Charlotte from the morning room. They found me, arms raised in front my face, standing stunned in the aftermath of the mirror's destruction, shards of glass still tinkling at my feet.

'What on earth has happened here?' said Charlotte, looking at the mirror and then at me. 'What have you done, Michael?'

'Me?' I said, lowering my arms. 'I've done nothing, I promise you.'

'Did the glass break itself then?' she said. 'Really. Is this how you repay Sir Stephen's kindness? That frightful nonsense yesterday and now this. I am surprised at you, Michael.'

'I didn't break the glass,' I said.

'Then who did?' she asked.

I looked at Charlotte and back to the glass strewn at my feet. I did not know what to say. I wasn't sure what I had seen. The anxiety induced by the reflection was still with me.

'There was something in the mirror,' I said. 'A boy.'

'A boy? A boy?' said Charlotte angrily. 'What silliness is this? The only boy in this house is you.'

'I did see him,' was all I could say.

'He's hurt, miss,' said Hodges, stepping forward.

It was then I noticed that blood was trickling down my face. One of the pieces of glass must have hit me when the mirror smashed.

'Why in heaven's name would you do such a thing, Michael?' said Charlotte, grabbing my arm tightly. 'I simply do not understand it. What am I to say to Sir Stephen?'

'Master Michael is hurt,' said Hodges more forcefully, pulling me away until she loosened her grip and stood looking dazed. 'I'll take him to the kitchen.'

Charlotte seemed to calm herself at Hodges' intervention.

'Very well,' she consented. 'Very well. See to him, Hodges.' Then, addressing me again, she said,

'Sir Stephen will be very disappointed.' With a slight quiver in her voice, she added, '*I* am very disappointed.'

With these words Charlotte straightened the folds of her dress, before turning on the spot and drifting off. Blood trickled into my eye, making her blur and shudder as she disappeared.

Hodges took me to the kitchen and Mrs Guston clapped her hands against her bosom, producing a cloud of flour behind which she all but disappeared.

'Lord above,' she gasped, coming towards us. 'Whatever has happened now? I heard such a terrible crash.'

'The mirror in the hall has smashed,' said Hodges matter-of-factly. 'Master Michael has a cut to his face. It is nothing serious, Mrs Guston. I know it isn't your area, but could I ask you to organise the tidying up of the glass while I see to Master Michael?'

'Of course,' she said, waving her hands in the air to reveal two large white handprints on her chest. 'Of course. Edith! Edith!'

With that, Mrs Guston took off to marshal the servants. Hodges soaked a piece of muslin in something from a brown bottle and held it to my forehead, making me wince.

'I should have mentioned that might sting, sir,' he said with a smile.

I smiled back.

'It's only a scratch,' he said. 'You'll be fine, sir. Hold that tight till it stops leaking.'

I sat by the fire and took hold of the swab of muslin and did as I was bidden. Hodges came and sat next to me. He poked at the coals for a few moments.

'What happened with the mirror, Master Michael?' Hodges asked. 'I know you didn't break it. What did you mean when you said there was a boy?'

'I don't know,' I said. Sure as I was of what I had seen, I knew how implausible it sounded.

Hodges looked at the floor and interlaced his fingers.

'Come now, Master Michael,' he said in a whisper. 'There's something happening here. I don't claim to know what it is, but there is certainly something. Jerwood told me that you heard banging behind the panelling of the priest hole. Is that why you went back there yesterday?'

'Yes,' I said, frowning. 'Not that anyone would believe me.'

Hodges gave me a long hard look.

'Sir Stephen hears banging,' he said. 'It's part of

his condition, the doctor says.' He leaned a little more towards me. 'But how can that be if you can hear it too?'

I didn't know how to respond to that.

Hodges shook his head.

'Why don't you tell me exactly what you saw in that mirror?'

I had been reluctant to agree at first, knowing how unbelievable it sounded. I had trouble believing it myself. But I now knew I was not alone in my experiences, and besides, there was relief to be had from sharing this burden, so I took it.

'I thought I saw a boy, but the mirror seemed to be twisting the reflection.' I frowned, trying to remember. 'No – only that part of it was twisted. There was a boy and then it was something else, something like a creature ...'

'A creature?' said Hodges. 'What sort of creature?'

'I can't say. Some strange thing,' I said. 'I ... I don't know what it was. It ... It climbed the wall like a great spider.'

Hodges looked as troubled by this account as though he had seen it with his own eyes.

'Sweet Jesus,' he muttered.

'So you believe me, Hodges?' I said.

'I don't know what to believe, Master Michael,'

he replied, grimacing. 'But I think I know a person's character well enough and I don't see you as a liar or a fool. And I know – we all do – that something is not right in this house.'

'Mr Jerwood said the priest hole had a special significance to Sir Stephen,' I said. 'What did he mean?'

I saw Hodges take a furtive glance towards Mrs Guston, who had just walked within earshot of our conversation. I saw too that she nodded in reply to his unspoken question.

'It's not right to speak ill of the dead, but Sir Stephen's father was a cruel man,' said Hodges. 'He was hard and brutal. He felt that his wife treated Miss Charlotte and Sir Stephen – and particularly Sir Stephen – with too much tenderness. He was obsessed with instilling some kind of toughness in him.

'But rather than making Sir Stephen tougher, he broke something in him: something that has never ever truly repaired itself.'

Hodges was lost in his memories for a moment.

'Tell the boy about what happened that Christmas,' said Mrs Guston, walking towards us.

'I was getting to that in my way, thank you, Mrs Guston,' said Hodges. 'And is that meant to be burning?'

Mrs Guston let out a shriek when she saw smoke drifting up from the oven and Hodges allowed himself a not unfriendly grin.

'As I was about to say, Michael,' said Hodges, 'it all came to a head one Christmas. Sir Stephen would have been your age. He'd been having a terrible time from his father. He used to lie in his room, sobbing, poor thing.

'I wasn't much older than him myself and I felt awfully sorry for him. My father was a good man, and kind. I couldn't understand how a father could treat his own son so badly.

'Then, that Christmas, it must have all become too much for him, because Sir Stephen's father walked into his study to find the whole place in a terrible state. Old Sir Stephen had been working on a history of his family and all his notes were strewn about the place and ripped into pieces. His books had been torn and spoiled.

'The young master made no attempt to hide the fact that he had done it and, for the first time anyone could remember, he stood up to his father and showed some courage.

'His father was furious. He dragged little Stephen kicking and screaming to the priest hole and threw him inside while his mother cried and begged her husband to be merciful.'

Hodges paused here and shook his head at the memory. When he looked back at me I was surprised to see tears in his eyes.

'Everyone at Hawton Mere knows the story of the priest hole, but it was only a little before this time that Sir Stephen's father had unearthed it while researching his book. The priest hole had been sealed and painted over and forgotten about for centuries. It would have been a mercy for everyone if it had stayed that way.

'It turned out that a Jesuit priest had hidden there when this house had been a Catholic stronghold. Queen Elizabeth's soldiers had come and taken the family into custody, but though they searched the house, they never did find the priest hole or the priest.

'No one knows why the priest didn't leave his hiding place. Maybe he was too scared. Maybe his mind had become unhinged. Whatever the reason, it was not until the family returned over a month later that the priest's body was found. They say his face was frozen in a look of terror, his fingernails broken as he had tried to claw his way free.

'In any event, Old Sir Stephen locked the young master in the priest hole and forbade anyone to go near the place. It was in the late afternoon and he did not allow his wife to release him until the following morning. Young Stephen hammered on those panels all night, poor little fellow.

'When his mother opened the priest hole, he came rushing out like a wild animal. She tried to comfort him and he attacked her. He scratched her face and knocked her to the floor. It took my father and two other servants to hold him still. And all the time he stared back towards the priest hole.'

I remembered my terror at being in that place – and that without knowing the terrible history of it – and had no difficulty understanding how Sir Stephen must have felt. I couldn't help but have some sympathy for him.

'Sir Stephen was never the same boy as he was before going in,' said Hodges. 'He has never been the same since. Father and son hardly exchanged a word after that and Sir Stephen took himself off into the army as soon as he could. He only came back for his father's funeral.'

Hodges swallowed as though tasting something particularly unpleasant.

'What kind of a man would do that to his own son? I remember it like it was yesterday, Master Michael. A thing like that etches itself on to your brain.'

He sighed and looked away towards the kitchen door.

'I think the evil of it has etched into the very stones of this house.

So it was with a heavy heart and with a goodly amount of trepidation that I made my way to the dining room that evening. But when I arrived I was relieved to find there was no sign of Sir Stephen, and at the end of the long table in that cavernous room was only one place setting, illuminated by a single candelabrum placed nearby.

The rest of the room was so shadowy I could barely perceive the extent of it, save for vague and ghostly glimpses of painted portraits looking out from the deep-red walls. A log fire burned in a huge hearth. An ornate, but faded, tapestry curtain hung across the wall opposite me.

Charlotte appeared through another door and told me that Sir Stephen was sadly still too unwell to meet me and would be eating in his room. I was to dine alone as she would be attending her brother and would eat later. With that, and her usual smile, she left.

CHAPTER ELEVEN

When I looked out of my bedroom on my return from dining I could not make out the moat below me any more, never mind the marsh beyond. It was like a solid mass – as if a high black wall had been constructed only inches from my window. The only thing I could see was my own troubled face reflected in the glass.

For all the friendly overtures of Hodges and Mrs Guston and Edith, still I was heartily sick of this house. I was forced to re-read the letter Bentley had given me from my mother entreating me to accept whatever help that Sir Stephen was willing to provide. Without it, I think I should have set off from that accursed place to take my chances on the open road.

Tiredness crept up on me, placing a heavy burden upon my shoulders, and my legs almost buckled under its weight. I washed and undressed and climbed into bed, happy to have the warmth of the bedclothes wrapped round me and eager for the oblivion of sleep.

Sleep came swiftly enough, but its hold over me was broken. I could not say what time it was I first heard the noise but, though I had cocooned myself in the bedclothes, not even the combined forces of pillows and blankets could block it out.

It had begun with a low moaning. Or at least that was when I first became aware of it. When I woke, my skin was already clammy with sweat and my heart racing. The moaning sounded both far off and close by: it was muffled as though through distance and yet it seemed to emanate from the very fabric of the walls. It resonated and vibrated through the stonework, moving by degrees from moan to plaintive wail to a terrible despairing screech. I should have said it was more like an animal, but I don't think an animal could ever produce a sound so pained and distraught.

It was so utterly dark I could not see the bed I lay upon, never mind the rest of the room. I stared out like a blind man, the sounds growing in volume, exaggerated by the stillness around me.

Surely that was a human voice? Surely that was a human cry?

As always with noises in the dark, it was difficult at first to discern from whence it came. I sat up in bed and threw away the covers, straining now to hear. There was a creak of floorboards and what sounded like breathing. There could be no doubt: someone was standing outside my door. This was confirmed when the door handle slowly turned.

'Hello?' I called. 'Who's there?'

The movement of the door handle immediately stopped. But though it remained motionless, I was sure that whoever had moved it was still outside, and so, as stealthily and silently as I could, I crept from my bed towards the door.

As I slowly made my way, arm outstretched, hand open, ready to grasp the handle, the sound of breathing grew louder in my ears and I fancied whoever it was out there stood, even then, with their face pressed up against the woodwork, listening.

I lunged to the door, grabbing the handle and

giving it a deft twist. I hardly knew what to antici-
pate as I flung wide the door. But I certainly did
not think to find no one there at all.

I leapt forward and into the passageway. I looked
left and right, peering into the darkness, but I could
see nothing and, though I held my breath to listen,
there was no sound either.

Could someone have run away so swiftly and
soundlessly? It seemed impossible. Yet I was convinced that, up until the moment I had opened the
door, there had been someone there.

A sudden recollection of Sir Stephen scurrying
away that morning, and of his wild behaviour
moments before, came to me as I stood staring into
the blackness and I shuddered. Was it he who
roamed these passages at night?

I went back into the room to retrieve the lamp
that burned by my bedside and came back into the
passageway. Holding it out in front of me, and
looking again in both directions, I once more confirmed that the passageway was certainly empty.

I began to feel somewhat foolish and had a
sudden dread of being caught in that position there
by Charlotte or one of the servants. I did not want
to have to explain what I was doing. Darkness
breeds doubt, and my certainties over the sounds

outside the door had already begun to collapse.

I returned to my room and closed the door behind me. But no sooner had I done so than I distinctly heard footsteps, fleet and short-paced.

The footsteps were running now, running along the passageway, faster and faster, back and forth past my door.

'Hello?' I whispered. 'Who's there?'

I had said these words in as friendly a way as is possible, albeit with a shakiness borne of nerves. But as I laid my fingers on the handle once again, the door was shaken by pounding of such violence that I almost fell backwards as I recoiled.

The panels buckled and the wood of the frame sounded ready to split, creaking and groaning like the planks of a ship in a storm. The very grain of the wood seemed to squeal. The hinges clattered and shook. Instinctively I leapt forward and turned the key in the lock.

The door handle began to rattle and turn back and forth, back and forth, until suddenly all was silent. I slowly released the breath I had been holding, and then, with equal suddenness, there was the sound of footsteps once again, running away this time. Summoning what little courage I had, I stepped forward and grabbed the door handle, startled by its coldness against my sweating palm. I turned the key and pulled the door open.

The moon must have risen above the clouds, for a little of its light seeped in through the small windows of the passage. I looked both right and left but could see nothing in either direction. I knew somehow that whoever had been there was there no longer.

I stepped back inside the room with some haste and lost no time in turning the key in its lock once more and taking it with me to place next to my bed. I lay down and covered myself again in bedclothes, but sleep did not come for quite some time and when I awoke my face was turned to the door as it had been when I finally succumbed.

CHAPTER TWELVE

I was awoken by Edith tapping at my door, and was surprised when I heard her walk in and gasp in astonishment. As I raised myself up to look at her, I saw anger on her face for the first time.

'Sir!' she said crossly. 'What have you done?'

'Done?' I said blearily. 'Whatever's the . . .'

But then I saw what it was had made Edith so vexed. The floor was strewn all about with spare bedding from the blanket box, my clothes and all manner of things, as if a whirlwind had passed through the room.

'It's me that will have to clear this up,' said Edith

tightly. 'If Miss Charlotte sees it . . .'

She began to sob. It took me a few moments to gather my thoughts. My door had been locked. The key was still where I had put it the night before. How? How?

'I shall clear it up, Edith,' I said. 'I promise. Miss Charlotte won't have anything to complain of.'

'I suppose it was a fine joke to play on me, then,' she said between sobs.

'It wasn't a joke,' I said. 'I'm sorry, Edith. Truly.'

Edith sighed.

'I shall come back later when you're at breakfast, sir,' she said, and hurriedly left.

Though I stared at the litter around the room in horrible wonder for some minutes, by the time I had tidied up and got dressed to go down to breakfast I had calmed myself a little. I had hoped to wake up to the realisation that I had simply fallen asleep after going to bed exhausted and dreamt the whole thing. It certainly had the flavour of a nightmare.

But it had clearly not been a dream. Somebody had been outside my door. Somebody had tried the handle. Somebody had run away before I could catch them. Somebody had come back when I was asleep and done this to my room. The idea of someone there when I was asleep was horrible.

I walked down the stairs and into the hall as Charlotte appeared from the drawing room. She moved towards me with her usual silent grace. She was wearing a dress of deepest blue and of a satin sheen and it shimmered like sunlit water as she moved.

'I trust you slept well, Michael,' she said, clicking her fingernails together rhythmically.

'I'm afraid not,' I said, still reeling from the sight that had greeted me.

'I'm sorry to hear that,' she said, laying a stiff hand on my shoulder. 'Are you not comfortable here?'

What was I to answer to a question like that? I smiled as best as I could and said, 'Yes, of course.'

'I hope we did not disturb you in the night?' she asked.

'I don't think so . . .' I said, wondering what she could mean.

'I'm afraid that Sir Stephen was taken ill again,' she said. 'He was very agitated indeed. He was so looking forward to your visit, Michael, but I fear you may see little of him during the remainder of your stay.'

That would hardly present a problem to me, I

thought to myself, and yet it made a mockery of his insistence that I be in that house over Christmas. What difference did it make to him?

Charlotte wished me a pleasant breakfast – she rarely took breakfast, she assured me – and glided down the passageway towards the archway that led to Sir Stephen's rooms in the tower.

I wondered again if it could have been Sir Stephen who was at my door. Was his mind so fractured and disturbed that he roamed the house at night? I thought of the wild man who had screamed and raved outside the priest hole. It wasn't difficult to imagine. Perhaps he had another key to my room.

I pictured him stooped over me with his clutching hands . . . Who knew what he was capable of when in that state? All these questions and more buzzed in my head like angry bees as I walked down to the dining room.

It was a fine morning and bright sunlight did its utmost to puncture the gloom of the house and light my way to breakfast. A number of the windows in the passageway contained fragments of stained glass and these cast a tinted glow on the opposite walls, painting them red, blue and gold. The colour seemed wrong – lurid, almost sickly – in that sombre house of shadows. I was again left to entertain myself as best I could that day.

This was no easy task in a place as unwelcoming as Hawton Mere, and the hours dragged by. I longed to talk to somebody. I needed to voice my troubled thoughts, to share them. To my surprise, it was Jerwood who came most readily to mind as a confidant, but in any case he was no longer in the house and I had no idea when I might see him again. I also would have liked an opportunity to discover more of what he knew of the mysterious woman, for it was clear that he was hiding something.

I thought too of the kindly Bentleys, and how warm and inviting their house would be right now, and how normal. In fact the portly, jolly Bentleys seemed a positive antidote to joyless Sir Stephen and this dismal place. I winced at how cold I had been to Bentley in return for his kindness and vowed to make amends the next time we met.

After much aimless wandering and many, many games of solitaire, it was time for lunch, which at least was a short affair of cold meats and pie. Charlotte joined me for this meal. I had been concerned that she would still be angry with me over the breaking of the mirror, but, whether she now accepted I was not to blame or had simply chosen to put it behind us, she made no further mention of the incident and betrayed no hint of lingering annoyance. In fact she seemed to make more than her usual effort to engage me in conversation. But I had come to the conclusion that she was one of those people who feel uncomfortable in the company of children. I was sure that she meant well enough, but it was more like an interview with a well-meaning schoolmistress and I was not upset when she apologised again and said she must attend to some important correspondence.

An afternoon of quiet tedium followed. I walked from room to room once more, looking again at the animal heads and stuffed birds, the paintings and books. I even stood at the top of the steps leading down to the priest hole.

All was silent there now and, though I could not have made myself walk down them for all the tea in China, I could sense that a large part of whatever horror had haunted that place was there no longer. Equally I knew that whatever that was, it was not gone from this house.

The boredom of these wanderings was alleviated by chance meetings with servants. Unlike Charlotte and Sir Stephen, they seemed genuinely pleased to have a young person about the house, and perhaps happy for an excuse to break off from their chores. They would talk and joke with me and tell me a little of themselves and of life in the village.

On my way back to my room with yet another book from the library, I passed the door to the balcony room and thought I might try the handle again. I reached out, but no sooner had my hand touched it than a voice made my heart leap in my chest.

'That room's always locked.'

It was Edith coming up the stairs.

'I just wondered what room it was,' I said.

'That was Her Ladyship's room,' said Edith. 'Sir Stephen likes it kept just as it was.'

I nodded and went on my way. I had learned whose room it was but little else. The mystery of the place remained intact and I settled down on my bed to read my book.

When it was once again time for dinner, I was not surprised to hear that Sir Stephen was still too ill for any company but Charlotte's and so she would take her meal with him in his study.

I was left alone to wonder what the two of them were talking about up in his tower. Did they talk about me and, if they did, what did they say? What did Sir Stephen have in store for me? What secrets lay at the heart of Hawton Mere? Having little but these ruminations to entertain me throughout my meal, my eyes rested upon the large tapestry hanging as a curtain at the far end of the room. It was an elaborate creation, filled with branches of foliage on which sat all manner of birds and animals.

It suddenly occurred to me during the study of this decorative curtain that there really ought to be no window in that wall, as it surely backed on to the entrance hall. A door perhaps? But I did not recall seeing a door on the corresponding wall in the hall. If the door had been filled in, then why hang a curtain there?

Perhaps I would have been less intrigued had I not been so eager to rid my mind of all thoughts of the night's adventures, but I decided to investigate.

I stood up slowly, putting my cutlery down and scraping back my chair. Edith, who was clearing away plates, started at the sound and stood watching me, but I paid her no heed. I walked to the curtain and pulled it aside.

Instead of a window or a door, the curtain concealed a large, life-sized portrait of a woman: a woman I recognised all too well, despite the fact that I had only glimpsed her once before. Though the woman in the portrait was dressed in expensive clothes and looking a figure of perfect health, I would have known her anywhere.

I stood there utterly transfixed, unable to make any sense of what I was seeing. The maid standing nearby saw my puzzled, pained expression.

'Bless you, sir,' she said. 'She was so beautiful, wasn't she, Lady Clarendon, poor thing. And not just in her looks, if you take my meaning. We all miss her terrible, God rest her soul.'

'Lady Clarendon?' I said.

'Yes, sir,' Edith answered, getting a little flustered at my evident perplexity and startled manner. 'It's on account of that portrait that Sir Stephen has taken to eating in his room, sir. But he won't have it removed.'

She chattered on as she left the room, but I was deaf to the words. Lady Clarendon? She was dead. How could that be Lady Clarendon? I had seen her with my own eyes.

What in heaven's name was happening here? Each secret seemed to have a secret of its own; each shadow hid another shadow darker than the first.

I walked back to my room with a quickening

step, trying to make sense of what had been said. But there seemed no sense to be made of it. I had only glimpsed the woman on the track. Perhaps I had been mistaken. And even if there had been a resemblance, still it did not mean that it was her. She could be some relative perhaps. But why would a relative of Lady Clarendon be roaming the marshes?

I returned to my room and walked across to the window to close the curtain. The moon had yet to rise and the marsh beyond the moat was invisible beneath the all-embracing blackness. Somewhere beyond, an owl shrieked.

The only illumination in the whole scene was two pale patches on the other side of the moat, where the light from my window, and that of another further along towards the tower, hit the earth.

All my confidence in the rational seemed to evaporate as I looked out. For I somehow knew she was going to appear; some secret sense let me know that she was there and, sure enough, she stepped into the light cast from that other window I surmised must be on the same floor as mine.

She slowly raised her head to look at the room from which the light came and, where I had once been full of pity for her, I was now overcome with dread. How could I ever have seen her as being alive? She was as ethereal as the mist that swirled about her, always on the verge of dissolving into it.

More than that, her posture suggested fear and trepidation. She stood with all the timidity of a deer, as if the slightest sound or movement from the house would send her fleeing into the marshes.

I pressed my face against the window, my breath coming short and fast, fogging the cold pane of glass. I wiped the mist away with my sleeve and, as I did so, the ghost turned her face and looked straight at me.

The expression she wore was startling. Her eyes opened wide and her mouth moved as she seemed to talk to herself. Her gaze filled me with horror and I could not for a moment understand why she was staring at me with such strange longing. And then it came to me: it was not simply that she could see me; it was that she had realised that I could see *her*.

I closed the curtain. I could not hold her gaze.

Was it she who tried my door last night? I backed away slowly from the window, staring at it. What kind of place was this where the dead roamed among the living?

I don't know how long I stood there, but eventually my legs felt so tired I feared they would not support me. I retired to my bed, leaving the lamp lit, a terrible phobia of that over-powering darkness having come upon me as I lay looking out towards the window.

CHAPTER THIRTEEN

And so it was Christmas Eve. I awoke to the sound of knocking and immediately felt my whole body tense with the same fear and trepidation that I had felt the previous night.

But it was only Edith. I stared at her with profound relief and my expression must have amused her because I saw she blushed at being looked at so intently.

'You must have been dog tired, sir,' said the maid.

'Sorry, Edith?'

'You forgot to turn your lamp off, sir.'

I nodded sheepishly, embarrassed by both the

show of fear it might reveal and by the waste of oil.

'I'll just go fetch you some warm water,' she said, picking up the jug from the washstand.

As Edith got to the door, she put her hand on the handle but did not turn it. She looked back at me as I stretched and yawned.

'Are you quite recovered from your accident, Master Michael?' she asked.

'It was just a scratch. I'm fine, thank you, Edith,' I replied.

She blushed and hurried from the room. As soon as she left, it felt suddenly colder and I lost no time in getting dressed and going downstairs for breakfast.

I ate staring ahead at the tapestry curtain hanging at the other end of the room, and as soon as I had finished I could not resist walking over to it and pulling it aside to reveal the portrait.

My heart skipped a beat as I did so. Although it was an almost unrecognisably healthy and well-dressed version of the woman I had seen outside the previous night, still it was so clearly the same person.

The liveliness and vigour that the painting portrayed was so utterly different to the lifeless thing that walked these marshes. What did she want with me? What could she possibly want with me?

I was walking back to my room after breakfast, when Charlotte slid out from the shadows by the doorway that led to Sir Stephen's tower wearing a deep green velvet dress, the colour of wet moss.

'Michael,' she said with a warm smile.

'Yes, Charlotte?'

'Sir Stephen wishes to speak to you.'

'He does?' I replied.

'Yes,' said Charlotte. 'He wants to talk to you – in private. He is in his study waiting for you. I shall take you to him.'

I nodded but was suddenly tongue-tied. *In private!* I was filled with trepidation about being left alone with my unpredictable guardian. Charlotte moved closer and placed a hand on each of my shoulders.

'I love my brother, Michael,' she said. 'I only seek to protect him. If that makes me seem harsh sometimes, then I apologise.'

I was about to say that there was no need, when she continued.

'I would ask you not to excite Sir Stephen unduly, Michael.'

'I will try not to,' I said, more than happy to comply.

'Very well. Come along,' she replied, turning and walking away.

I followed Charlotte and we entered that part of the house from which the tower sprouted. It was clear even to my untrained eye that we had entered a much more ancient part of the building.

Charlotte set off up a spiral staircase formed of great slabs of stones, whose walls were rough and bulging here and there with outcrops of rock and flint. It was dark and dank and a little dizzying as we climbed its vortex.

Eventually we came to a landing of sorts and a small arched doorway as one might find at the base of a church tower, formed of oak panels and studded with nail heads.

Charlotte grasped the metal hoop that held the latch and knocked three times, the sound tumbling down the stone steps. A muffled voice answered from inside and she lifted the latch and opened the door. She did not enter though, but merely smiled at me and edged past, disappearing back down the stairs and leaving me alone in the doorway.

'Come in, Michael,' came the voice again.

I walked through the door and was immediately taken aback by the scale of the room, which occupied the whole width of the tower and soared upwards to a vaulted ceiling high above. Massive and well-stocked bookshelves lined the walls, an ancient globe stood nearby and there was a large telescope by the window. A huge hearth contained a modest fire before which sat Sir Stephen, in an extraordinarily grotesque high-backed chair, a book open on his lap.

'Michael,' he said, standing up as I entered the room. He was taller than I had realised from my previous encounter with his wilder self, though he was dressed identically in black from head to foot. His face was gaunt and pale and, all in all, he would have made a most acceptably sombre undertaker.

'Come and sit down,' he said. 'Are you finding enough ways to amuse yourself at Hawton Mere? Charlotte has introduced you to the library, I gather?'

'Yes, sir,' I said. 'Charlotte has been very kind.'

We both sat by the fire. Sir Stephen seemed restless. His left hand was in a constant state of agitation. The long fingers ended in long nails and they scratched and picked at the fabric of his trousers at the thigh. I could see that the area was worn and threadbare. His right hand would make occasional trips across to try and stop it, grabbing the wayward hand at the wrist.

'Charlotte told me about the incident with the mirror,' said Sir Stephen, so quietly it was almost as though he was speaking to himself.

'I did not break it, sir,' I said. 'Honestly I –'

Sir Stephen put his hand up to silence me.

'No need, Michael,' he said. 'No need to explain. I have not brought you here to chastise you about that mirror. I have always hated it. I shall not miss it.'

My guardian leaned forward, resting his long hands on his knees. The firelight twinkled in his eyes.

'But I am intrigued,' he said. 'If you did not break the mirror, then who did?'

'It . . . It just broke,' I said. 'On its own.'

Sir Stephen nodded, as if this information was simply what he had expected and nothing more.

'And did you *see* anything before it happened?' he said.

My first impulse was to tell him the truth, as I had done with Hodges, and yet I could not help but recall Charlotte's plea for me to show some under-standing of Sir Stephen's mental state and do nothing to unnecessarily excite him.

'No, sir,' I said.

Sir Stephen smiled unpleasantly.

'You are sure?' he said. 'You saw nothing at all?'

'No, sir,' I answered again.

'And you have seen and heard nothing unusual during your stay at Hawton Mere?'

'No, sir,' I said.

Sir Stephen looked at me for a long time, saying nothing, and his gaze was horribly unsettling, like the stare of a praying mantis before it strikes.

'Come on!' he said, getting suddenly to his feet. 'Let's get some air.'

Sir Stephen strode across to an arched doorway between two bookshelves and disappeared. Feeling nervous but a little foolish at being left behind, I felt I had no choice but to follow him.

The doorway concealed another staircase going up. The walls and the spiralling steps were made of bricks and were so small that there was barely room to put one's whole foot upon them and I had to climb them almost on tiptoe.

A wooden door greeted me at the summit and, opening it, I found that we were on the leaded roof of the tower, to one side of the little tiled spire. Sir Stephen was standing at the battlemented edge, looking down. I walked over to join him and he started at my approach as if he had quite forgotten me.

He recovered his wits enough to beckon me over. He was wearing a pair of strange round spectacles. They were tinted deep blue; I could not see his eyes. He noticed that I was looking at them.

'I have developed an aversion to light,' he said, seeing my expression. 'It is quite a view, is it not, Michael?'

I had to confess it was. The land was so flat for miles around that the vista seemed endless, the horizon as white and flat as a frozen ocean – as though we stood in the crow's nest of a ship trapped in ice.

'My forefathers built this house for its strategic value – the marshes and the moat are its protection. But it doesn't make the house very hospitable.

'I was born here,' he continued. 'I played in the courtyard as a child. My sister and I ran about this house. When my father was away, there was occasionally laughter, even joy.'

I tried, unsuccessfully, to imagine either Sir Stephen or Charlotte as happy, laughing children.

'I used to play with Hodges,' said my guardian with a loud laugh. 'Think of it! We were inseparable. We still are, I hope, though things perforce have changed between us. But he is a good man, Michael. Don't be taken in by that gruff exterior.'

'I never doubted it,' I replied, though this was not quite true.

'Charlotte used to play with us as well, I think,' Sir Stephen went on, giving himself up to the memories. He took off his tinted spectacles and rubbed his eyes, trying to remember.

'No, no,' he said, replacing his glasses. 'I can't recall.'

He looked back down at the courtyard.

'Ah, Charlotte,' he said. 'Where would I be without her strength? Where? She is too devoted, I often think. I know that she feels she cannot leave me, and yet I worry that I have stopped her from partaking of life's joys – a husband, a family.' At these words Sir Stephen's smile disappeared and he turned to stride across to the other side of the tower, standing with his back to me as he stared out across the marshes. The sky was now an ominous grey and the wind felt chill.

'We have a good deal in common, Michael, you and I,' he shouted, without turning round.

'Sir?' I replied, wondering at how he might have reached such a conclusion.

'You and I have known great sadness,' he said. 'I also lost my mother when I was still relatively young, and I thought I should never know such pain again, but it was eclipsed when I lost my dear wife.'

He turned to face me as I approached him. His long face looked even paler now against the darkening sky and his tinted spectacles created the illusion of eyeless sockets.

'She was such a lovely creature,' he said. 'So warm. So *happy*.' He gave the word 'happy' a peculiar stress, as if he were describing an exotic spice. 'She seemed to have an inexhaustible supply of happiness and, for a while, I didn't feel the dejection that had plagued my youth. But all happiness is finite, Michael.'

I needed no reminding of that! He turned back to gaze between the battlements, staring up at the sky as though looking for something. He took a small bottle from his pocket, removed the stopper and took a swig.

'Laudanum,' he said, as he put it back in his pocket. 'Dr Ducharme does not approve, but Dr Ducharme can go to hell.'

Sir Stephen looked at the lead beneath his feet for a moment and then back to me.

'Do you sleep, Michael?' he inquired suddenly.

'Here, sir, do you mean?' I asked, a little puzzled.

'I rarely do,' he said.

He lurched towards me.

'They think I'm mad, you know. Because I hear things. But you hear things too, don't you, Michael?' He peered into my face. 'Don't you?'

And it was then that, for all Charlotte's urging, I was suddenly struck by the simple fact that Sir Stephen deserved to know the truth. I knew what it was like to be disbelieved and it seemed unfair to pretend that I was also deaf to those noises.'

'Yes, sir,' I said.

Sir Stephen smiled. 'Thank you,' he said. 'Thank you. So like your father.'

He stared at me strangely, and I could see my own reflection in his tinted glasses.

'It has escaped, you know,' he said matter-of-factly. 'It used to be simply noises. The noises were dreadful enough. But now sometimes I think I see it in the shadows.'

There was the sudden noise of pattering feet, as if a child had just run across the roof, and Sir Stephen wheeled round in a panic. I could almost see his heart pounding beneath his coat. One or two flakes of snow floated past on the chill breeze. I was about to tell Sir Stephen that I had seen Lady Clarendon's ghost, when he grabbed hold of my arm.

'I thought it would be a relief to know I was not

mad,' he said, 'to know that someone else could share these horrors with me. But now I find that they are real, it frightens me all the more. Madness seems attractive now.'

He laughed at this and pulled me towards him.

'What say we jump, Michael?' he said. 'Eh?'

I wriggled away from him and he laughed, climbing up so that he now stood on the edge.

'Just me, then?' he said, glancing at me over his shoulder as he teetered on the brink, and I saw that he meant to do it.

'No!' I shouted. 'My father died to save your life. Don't you dare waste it!'

I shocked myself with the vehemence of these words and my voice seemed to split the cold air like a whip-crack. Sir Stephen took a deep breath, hung his head and climbed down. I had tears in my eyes, more from fury than from sadness.

'You are quite right, of course,' said Sir Stephen. 'Your father was a very brave man. He was a good soldier. He fought well and he cared about his men.

'I was a poor officer, as you can imagine, Michael. I was only there to please my father. How many men died because of my incompetence? I wonder. It would have been better for everyone if the bullet that struck your father had struck me instead.'

I felt in no mood to argue with this sentiment as it happened to be a perfect summary of my own feelings on the subject. The snow was falling more steadily now, in fat woollen flakes.

'But I am to make amends to some degree,' he said, looking at me earnestly.

I frowned, wondering if this was more lunacy. I desperately wanted to get away from this strange man. I was about to make my excuses when Sir Stephen slapped his hands together loudly.

'Run along now, Michael,' he said, stroking his lank white hair, flakes of snow settling on his coat. 'I must not detain you any longer.'

With that he turned away from me and stood gazing out across the land once again. I stood a moment looking at his thin black shape, a beetle on its back legs, and wondered if he was thinking about jumping again.

But that particular madness seemed to have passed and he appeared quiet now. I left him and returned by the narrow stairs, finding Charlotte at the foot about to come up, tapping her fingernails against the plaster wall.

'Ah, I was just coming to find you. You have been talking with Sir Stephen for some time,' she said. 'I hope you haven't tired him out.'

'I don't think so,' I said.

'Is everything all right?' she asked.

'Yes, quite all right.' I wondered if I ought to tell her of Sir Stephen's threat to jump from the tower, but decided against it. I was sure that nothing I could tell her would come as any surprise. She knew what her brother was like and I certainly didn't want to attract any blame for having agitated him. Besides, I felt a sudden rush of sympathy for her and had no wish to worry her further.

'Well, excuse me, then, Michael.'

I moved aside and she climbed the stairs to her brother. I eagerly returned to my room and the warmth of the fire.

CHAPTER FOURTEEN

I needed to get out of that hateful place. More and more I felt like a prisoner in Hawton Mere, and those imposing grey walls felt, day by day, more and more like high prison walls. To be fair, I had not been forbidden to leave the confines of the house. It was a self-imposed incarceration, for I had a fear of both those dreary marshes and the ghost who haunted them.

My spirits were revived a little when I looked out of my window some hours later and saw that the snow that had been falling steadily since my meeting with Sir Stephen had settled thickly. All the wide sweep of land thereabouts was covered in such a thick white blanket that the house now appeared to soar above the clouds, and for a moment my soul felt as though it had taken flight along with it.

Nothing lifts the mood like new-fallen snow. I can think of no ills that would not be lightened by two or three well-aimed snowballs. I wanted nothing more than to get out of that dismal house and run out into that gleaming whiteness. I decided to explore the island on which Hawton Mere was standing.

To one side of the house was a garden, part of which was formal, with clipped yews standing like pieces in an abandoned game of chess – albeit a giant one. The other part was a kitchen garden, from which Mrs Guston got many of her vegetables and herbs. There were chickens too, and a hen-house for them to live in.

Where the moat widened to a kind of lake, there was a boathouse with a rowing boat, though both looked in a sorry state of neglect. Nearby, a huge wooden buttress was stacked against the old walls like a bookend.

But I soon exhausted the possibilities of this island, and I decided that I must once more cross the moat and get some space and good air about me. The snow now carpeted the marshes and it seemed a new place, brighter and less threatening – much less threatening than the house that towered over me. I crossed the bridge and instantly felt as though I could breathe more freely.

It was a cold morning. The sky was now lined with a thin coating of cloud and occasionally snow would once again fall in fitful flurries. Clarence joined me, though he soon grew bored and, after chasing a passing magpie, he trotted back towards the house.

I busied myself in the construction of a snowman, whose rotund features put me happily in mind of good old Mr Bentley. After its completion I decided to walk the whole circuit of the moat and then head back into the house where I would warm my toes in front of the fire in the kitchen.

Hawton Mere looked as massive as ever. I found myself stopping and staring up at Sir Stephen's spire-topped tower, wondering about the man inside and just what part he had played in the tragic events at the house. Was it grief or remorse that laid him low? Was it guilt that held him prisoner here?

I rounded the whole house, edging past the

bloated part of the moat. The ground near the water became more uneven and swamp-like with the frosted and blackened leaves and seed heads of reeds and bulrushes. I was forced further out into the surrounding marsh, stepping from hummock to hummock in avoidance of the frozen bog between.

I eventually made my way back to the bridge and walked beyond it to stand beneath the window to my room. As I did so I realised that when I saw Lady Clarendon's ghost, she was staring up intently at a certain part of the house and I had a suspicion what that might be.

I walked back towards the bridge a few yards until I stood where I thought she had stood and looked up. There was the stone balcony, with an arched door leading on to it – the same place I had imagined seeing something fall.

As I stood there gazing up at it, I heard a strange noise nearby. It began with a sound like chalk on a wet slate: a squeaking and squealing as the ice in front of me began to crack. The noise was so high-pitched that it was painful to hear and I placed my hands over my ears to shut it out.

Looking down at the moat I saw something loom up out of the filthy depths of the water and up towards the thick ice. It was just a shape at first, a darkness in among the icy grey, but then it came into focus. Lady Clarendon's face stared up at me from beneath the ice, not with wildness or with anger, but with a look of overwhelming sadness.

I was filled with a stupefying terror. I could do nothing but stand and gape at this pitiful creature: pitiful but dreadful all the same, her skin blue-white, her limpid eyes red-rimmed under the layer of ice.

I had an instant to take in her terrible, pale and tragic form: her wet hair floating beside her face, her hands reaching up towards the ice above her. And then it happened ...

I heard the faintest whispering behind me, as if a snake were sliding across the snow. The pressure on my back was almost imperceptible at first. It was like a breeze that gained in power with appalling suddenness until it shoved me forward, my shoes slithering at the snowy moat's edge and my whole body sliding, slipping, falling feet first into the ice.

The cold hit me like a kick from a carthorse, knocking the wind from my lungs and making it difficult to breathe as I tried and failed to gain purchase on the ice, which broke away at my touch, or upon the muddy bank. My clothes were so heavy with water; it was as though an anchor had been bound to my legs, for I struggled to keep even my upturned face above the water.

My attempts to shout for help were pitiful. The cold and the fear had squeezed my lungs dry and I suddenly felt sure that this was my death: this was how I was to die. I was wheezing painfully now, the walls of the house high above me swirling in and out of view as I flailed around in desperation.

All struggle spent, I could no longer keep my face afloat and as I sank beneath the black and icy waters of the moat I sensed my soul was already free and swimming away from me. It was like sleep and it did not feel so terrible.

But suddenly I felt something grab me and drag me back from that watery fate. It seemed to take an age, as if I had already sunk to unfathomable depths and was being hauled up by rope.

And then light and sound exploded all around me. The walls of the house were there once more, then gone, then towering over me again. Then a face loomed in front of me, blurred. A voice was calling my name. A dog – Clarence! – was barking excitedly.

I felt so cold. I was lifted to my feet but I could not feel my legs to stand, and doubled over, vomiting a copious amount of the foul-tasting moat water into the snow at my feet.

Powerful arms lifted me off the ground and began to walk with me towards the bridge. My head lolled backwards drunkenly and standing, just faintly visible at the mist's edge, was the ghost, watching my departure.

I raised my head to see who my rescuer was and the unmistakable craggy profile of Hodges came into focus.

'We must get you to the house, Master Michael,' he said, 'and get you warm.'

He carried me with no discernable effort and I felt like a small child again. I had a strange half-memory of my father carrying me like this when I was very small and the thought of it, and the misery of my condition, brought tears to my eyes.

Hodges ran up the steps and kicked the door open. Edith was dusting in the hallway and looked terrified at our approach. I was more concerned that she had seen me crying and raised my arm to shield my face.

'Hold that door open and fetch Mrs Guston, girl,' shouted Hodges, making for the kitchen.

Edith snapped into action, running to open the door for us, then followed after, shouting for the cook as Hodges took me over to the fire. When Edith came back with Mrs Guston, the cook shrieked with horror and told Edith to get blankets.

I had not appreciated just how cold I had become until I entered the warmth of the kitchen. My whole body was now stinging painfully as though it were studded all over with rose thorns. My skin was a pale blue; a corpse would have looked livelier.

Mrs Guston clucked and fussed about me as if I were a small child and I was happy to acquiesce. Tears welled in my eyes as my shoes and wet britches were taken and I was wrapped in a huge blanket by the roaring fire.

'Fetch the lad some hot milk, Mrs Guston,' said Hodges. 'And a nip of brandy wouldn't go amiss. I'll have a glass myself.'

'What is going on?'

Charlotte drifted in. She had changed her dress again.

'Master Michael slipped while out walking, ma'am,' said Mrs Guston. 'Mr Hodges pulled him out of the moat –'

'Heaven be praised,' said Charlotte, rushing forward. She gathered me up in a warm embrace and when she let me go I saw there were tears in her eyes. 'You are not to go out there again. You are to go nowhere near that moat. You could have been killed. Oh, Michael, Michael. Promise me you will stay away from that moat.'

'Yes, ma'am,' I replied hoarsely.

'Edith!' said Hodges, making the girl jump an inch or two in the air. 'Don't stand there gawping, girl. There's work to do. And that goes for all of you!'

He clapped his hands with a crack like a rifle shot and we all started at the sound and breathed once more. Then Hodges followed Charlotte out of the kitchen.

I looked about me at the servants but no one seemed to want catch the eye of another and so I turned to the fire and watched the dancing flames. The warmth of the fire without, and the hot milk and brandy within, slowly did their work, and I fancied Death might have to come looking for me another day.

CHAPTER FIFTEEN

Dry clothes were brought for me and the kitchen cleared of prying eyes so that I could change with some privacy. All the same I got undressed and redressed with the greatest possible haste, horribly concerned that Edith or Mrs Guston or Charlotte would wander in as I was halfway through the exercise.

I need not have worried however. After a goodly amount of time, there was a knock at the door and Mrs Guston's smiling face appeared.

'All done, then?' she asked.

I said that I was ready and she breezed in

followed by Edith, who, on Mrs Guston's instructions, picked up my soaking wet clothes and
carried them off. I decided to go back to my room, a
little exhausted at being quite so on display.

Edith had banked up the fire in my bedroom and
I pulled a chair in front of it and sat cherishing the
heat. My bones still felt chilled and I was in no
hurry to move. While I sat there toasting my feet,
there was a knock at the door and Hodges walked
in.

I made as if to stand up, but he raised his hands
to stop me.

'You don't get up for me,' he said.

'I never thanked you for saving my life,' I said.

'I was glad to do it,' he replied. 'Though it's
Clarence you really have to thank.'

'Really?' I said with raised eyebrows. 'How?'

'I'd never have heard you, sir,' said Hodges. 'These
walls are so thick, you can't hear a thing from one
side of the house to the other. No – it was Clarence
who heard and it was Clarence who started barking
and howling and told me something was amiss. You
can't spend too long in water that cold without
going under for good. A few more seconds and it
would have been too late.'

Hodges broke off here and looked into the fire

and I saw him swallow dryly.

'I wish to God that I could have got to Lady Clarendon as quickly.'

'Lady Clarendon?' I said. 'What do you mean?'

'Has no one told you, Master Michael?' said Hodges. 'That's how she died. She took her own life. She jumped into the moat, God bless her. What a way to go!'

So that was why her ghost was always dripping wet and why she haunted the moat's edge. I pictured poor Lady Clarendon's pallid features staring up at me from under the ice.

'I was too late for her, sir,' he continued. 'She was already dead when I pulled her out.'

The memory of fighting for purchase on those floating fragments of ice and the terrible blackness of the water came back to me in a surge and I shivered.

'It's a strange thing, sir,' said Hodges, as if he were talking to the fire.

'What is, Hodges?' I said.

He looked at me with great earnestness.

'The place you fell, sir,' he said. 'That was the self-same place Her Ladyship came down into the moat. The self-same place.'

I thought of the balcony and realised that it must

have been from there that Lady Clarendon had jumped. Hodges looked at me with intense scrutiny.

'I saw her, Hodges,' I said. 'I saw her under the ice before I fell.'

Hodges eyes brimmed full of tears and it was such a tragic sight in a man so rugged that I felt tears sting my eyes too.

I paused here, not quite knowing how to tell him about the other times without adding to his grief, but I felt he had to know the truth. When I had finished describing what I had seen, how I now knew it was Lady Clarendon I had seen on the road to Hawton Mere that first night, he hung his head and sobbed like a child.

After a few moments he took a deep breath and stood up, wiping his tears with the back of his hand.

'Is there anything you require, Master Michael?' he said, returning in an instant to his usual role.

'No thank you, Hodges,' I said.

'Then I will be on my way, sir,' he said with a small bow. 'Edith will come by from time to time to check on you. Good day, sir.'

'Thank you again, Hodges,' I said. 'For saving my life.'

He paused at the door and looked back at me.

'What does she want, Master Michael?' he asked.

It was a question I had already pondered myself.

'I don't know,' I replied.

And then he was gone.

Edith did indeed look in on me at regular intervals – possibly more regularly than strictly necessary – and though Charlotte had the doctor come and see me as he was at the house on one of his regular visits to Sir Stephen, I was not really in need of his services.

'You are a very lucky young man,' said the doctor in a strong accent, patting my shoulder after he had examined me. 'A very lucky young man indeed.'

'Are you French, sir?' I asked, knowing the answer already but feeling the need to have some conversation with the man.

'Oui,' he replied as he picked up his bag. 'Claude Ducharme at your service.'

'You're treating Sir Stephen?'

'Oui,' he said. 'I do my best.'

'How is he?' I asked.

Ducharme tapped his finger against his rather impressive nose. 'A doctor cannot talk of one patient with another, mon ami. All is private. All is secret.'

I nodded, assuming that would be the end of it, but Ducharme had not finished.

'In truth there is nothing wrong with the body,' he said. 'But some things are outside my expertise.'

'The mind, you mean?' I said.

'No, no,' replied Ducharme, slapping his hand against his heart. 'The soul, my young friend, the soul.'

Dr Ducharme walked towards the door and opened it. He turned and gave me a generous smile.

'For you, I prescribe that you stay near to a fire and stay warm – at least for the rest of the day. No more swimming!'

On that note, and clearly very pleased with his joke, Dr Ducharme left, closing the door behind him.

I followed his instructions to the letter, staying in my room near the fire and reading. Mrs Guston had some warm broth brought up to me and by the time I had finished it I was happy to go to my bed. The business of cheating Death was obviously more exhausting than I had thought and I was soon ready for sleep.

Once again I decided to leave my lamp lit and

suffer the embarrassment should Edith notice again. But this time I did not sleep through until morning; I woke instead in the dead of night.

I awoke in an instant, my whole body tensed to a danger I could not identify but knew to be present. The lamp left lit was now extinguished. The dark was impenetrable, as thick and black as ink. There was someone in the room. I held my breath and kept as still as possible.

In fact as I lay there, my heart pounding, I felt sure that I could sense someone standing beside my bed. Were they leaning towards me now? Was that their breath on my face?

I could restrain myself no longer and jumped up in the bed, recoiling.

As I sat hunched up, shivering, I began to wonder if I'd been mistaken, for there seemed to be no other sound in the room than my rapid breathing and shifting among the sheets and blankets. But then I heard it.

Across the other side of the room, there was a low and sorry sobbing. And it was clearly the sobbing of a child and, more precisely, of a boy, I was certain. There was something so plaintive and sad about the sound that all fear drained from me and I felt only compassion.

'Hello?' I said at last. 'Who's there?'

There was no response save that the sobbing died away for a few moments before restarting with even more heartbroken fervour.

'Who's there?' I said, trying to sound more confident than I felt. 'Please. Say something.'

The sobbing slowed and became more stifled and eventually reduced to a shallow breathing sound, interrupted now and then by sniffing and sighing that, in its turn, gave way to a rattling growl.

I think I knew then that I would receive no reply. For now I was certain the sound did not come from a person – a *living* person. While my own voice was perfectly normal, the other was hollow and echoed as if in a dungeon rather than my bedchamber.

I edged towards the glow of the fire – indeed it was the only light in the room, and so dim that at first I had not even registered it. I knew there were tapers in the hearth and, fumbling around, I found one, lit it on the embers and used its gentle illumination to light my way to the lamp at my bedside.

Oh, what a wonderful thing light is and how our ancestors must have cherished it. I felt something of their awe and wonder at the lift it gave my soul.

There was a sudden commotion as soon as I moved the light and a shadow scurried across the room. The door opened at its touch and it fled.

I followed with my lamp turned high and bright and held it in front of me to light the passageway, yet I saw nothing to the right or to the left.

I took some tentative steps along the corridor, the better to further my view, and all at once the very walls seemed to distort and bend outwards and a wind blew down the passageway – a warm wind like the fetid breath from some immense, vile invisible mouth. The lamp at once was snuffed out.

Pitiless darkness leapt upon me – and fear likewise. I could see nothing at all, and though I knew I was only inches from my door, my fumbling hands could not find it. I heard footsteps running towards me and I scratched at the wall in panic, finally laying hands on the door handle, leaping into my room and slamming the door behind me.

I stayed there for some time before I could move, the only sounds being my panting breath and pounding heart. Eventually I found the strength to lock the door, relight my lamp and climb into bed.

CHAPTER SIXTEEN

Edith came in and wished me 'Merry Christmas' with a blush, but I could barely register her visit I was so exhausted.

Merry Christmas! How many children would hear those words today and spring joyfully from their beds? Was it really Christmas Day? How normal it sounded.

'Merry Christmas, Edith,' I said quietly and she looked at me tenderly.

'Surely we can raise a smile from you on Christmas Day, sir?' she said cheerfully.

I smiled weakly back at her and she put down

the jug of hot water and busied herself with the fire, coaxing flames from the embers.

When she had left, I swung my legs round to put my feet on the floor. My legs felt shaky, as though I had run for miles and had fallen into bed exhausted.

I tottered over to the window and looked out at a world of snowy whiteness and, once again, the sight succeeded in lifting my spirits. I needed some fresh air.

I eagerly dressed, Edith having kindly lain my clothes before the fire, and ran downstairs, finding Hodges in the hall.

'Merry Christmas, Hodges,' I said, heading for my coat and boots.

'Breakfast first, young sir,' he said with a wry smile.

'I promise I will go nowhere near the moat,' I said. 'But I just want to get out into the snow and –'

'The snow will be there when you've finished.'

I rocked back and forth from heel to toe and looked at him pleadingly, but all he did was turn me round and point me towards the kitchen door.

I trudged across the hall. Hodges had not even seen the need to wish me a merry Christmas, I thought to myself, and was surprised at how much that hurt.

I must have looked a forlorn figure indeed as I opened the kitchen door, so unreservedly had I cast my soul down into a pit of self-pity. So the effect was all the more marked when I was met not only with a blast of heat as ferocious as a furnace, but also with a loud and hearty hail of greetings.

'Merry Christmas!' came a volley of voices, so unexpected as to make me jump back initially, before regaining my senses and grinning at the assembly of servants standing in the warm glow of the fire. Mrs Guston walked forward, arms extended, and gave me a bear hug.

'Merry Christmas, Master Michael,' she said.

Hodges walked up as she loosed her hold of me and patted me on the back. 'Merry Christmas, Master Michael.'

I wished the same in return and thanked them profusely and a little tearfully for their gathering to greet me in this way. They led me to a table where a special place had been set for me with holly and rosemary in a little pot – picked by Edith, I was told, much to the poor girl's embarrassment.

There, laid out for me, was a small collection of gifts. Edith had sewn my initials into one of my handkerchiefs with such delicacy I was quite over-whelmed. Mrs Guston had made me some biscuits tied up with a red bow and there was a small object wrapped in linen and tied with a green ribbon.

Hodges nodded and I picked it up and undid the ribbon to reveal a small wooden whistle that I could see Hodges had made himself. I was touched by the effort, knowing what a busy man he was, but somewhat baffled by the purpose of it.

'Thank you, Hodges,' I said, my confused face making him laugh. Edith looked as surprised as I was to hear that sound from him.

'Blow it,' said Hodges, and I could hardly refuse.

So, feeling a little self-conscious, I placed the whistle to my lips and blew. To my intense embar-rassment, no sound emerged. Poor Hodges. All that effort and the thing did not actually work. I was about to give the whistle another try, when there was a great galloping noise and Clarence burst in through the kitchen door.

'Mr Hodges!' shrieked Mrs Guston. 'I cannot have that animal in my kitchen!'

Hodges laughed and I joined him, as Clarence jumped up at me and licked my face.

'Blow that and he'll come running, have no fear.'

'Right now!' said Mrs Guston. 'Everybody who

ain't supposed to be here, out of my kitchen! And that means you especially, dog!' she shouted at Clarence.

I got up to leave, gathering my presents together and heading for the door. I don't think I could have stood that heat a moment longer in any case. 'Merry Christmas!' I called from the doorway.

Christmas Day! The house was quite changed. It may have been my mood, but not entirely. Hawton Mere was actually lively, with servants in their finest clothes rushing this way and that. The festive spirit could even enter a place such as this, I realised, and there was a lot of comfort in that thought.

When I next peeped into the kitchen, Mrs Guston was scurrying about, stirring pots and rolling pastry and barking orders to anyone in earshot, pausing only occasionally to mop her sweating brow with her sleeve. A confusion of aromas filled the air: cinnamon, cloves, apples, rosemary, bread and pastry, and the activity was dizzying. I decided to make myself scarce.

I stepped out into the courtyard just as a carriage rumbled in. It was the same carriage that brought me here. Jarvis pulled the horse to a stop and jumped down to open the door. To my surprise, out stepped Mr Jerwood, immaculately dressed as always.

'Michael,' he called as he stepped down. 'How are you, my boy?'

'I'm well, sir,' I said. 'And you?'

'Not bad,' Jerwood replied. 'Not bad, you know.'

'I'm very glad to see you back, sir.'

'Well, I thought you might appreciate a friendly face,' said the lawyer, and this seemed so like a joke at his own expense, given that he had such an unfriendly countenance, that I laughed. Much to my relief, he joined me.

'Jarvis told me about your accident in the moat, Michael.'

'Yes, sir, but I am quite recovered, as you see.'

'And here is the hero of the hour,' Jerwood said as Hodges approached.

'Only did what any man would,' said Hodges.

'Nonsense. You are a hero and the very best of men – isn't that right, Michael?'

'Yes, sir,' I said.

And I laughed, for no particular reason other than a desire to hear that sound again after so long.

CHAPTER SEVENTEEN

I walked with Jerwood up the stairs and we had not reached the top when he turned to me and whispered, 'We need to talk, Michael. Go to your room and wait for me there. I need to speak to Sir Stephen and Hodges and then I will be right there.'

I agreed to Jerwood's request and waited as patiently as I was able for his knock at the door. When it finally came, I opened the door and Jerwood came in, his face deadly earnest, and immediately sat by the fire, asking me to join him.

'I am a rational man, Michael,' he said quietly. 'I take pride in those words. Never in my wildest dreams did I ever imagine that I would be about to have the conversation I think we are to have.'

'Sir?' I said.

'Sir Stephen was not an altogether happy man even before Lady Margaret took her life, Michael,' Jerwood continued, 'though he was happier with her than I had ever seen him before. But I think a good deal of his unhappy state of mind can be traced back to that day, to the time he was locked in the priest hole. Hodges has told you about that, I gather.'

'Yes, sir,' I replied.

'The mind is a fragile thing, Michael,' he said as he walked over to the portrait of Sir Stephen on my bedroom wall. Jerwood breathed a sigh. 'I had never seen a person so wild and terrified as he was that day.'

'Do you mean to say you were here when it happened?' I asked.

'Yes,' he said. 'Before I was Sir Stephen's lawyer, I was his friend – and I hope I always shall be, however difficult that may be at times. We were at school together and though I was not at all of his rank or standing in the world, I had been invited to spend Christmas with him –'

'Just as I have been,' I interrupted.

Jerwood nodded.

'Just as you have been. I would have been about your age,' he added. 'As would Sir Stephen.'

Jerwood was lost to these thoughts for a few moments. Then he sat back down with his hands on his knees and leaned towards me. He made two or three attempts to start before he finally managed to get a coherent sentence out.

'Many years ago,' he said, 'Sir Stephen told me a curious story about your father.'

'My father?' I said, startled by this sudden change in topic.

'Yes,' said Jerwood. 'It happened some months before he was killed – while he and Sir Stephen were together in Afghanistan.

'Sir Stephen's regiment were resting at a small village, waiting for the big push into Kabul. Of course, the locals were hostile but, intimidated by the force of numbers, they could do little except to put on a show of accommodating them with reasonable hospitality. The officers were billeted in a large deserted palace.

'On the first night Sir Stephen saw your father standing in the moonlit courtyard, staring into space. He called to him and had to call twice before your father responded. Sir Stephen asked him what

163

he had been looking at. "The boy by the well," replied your father. But Sir Stephen couldn't see a boy.

'He happened to mention this to one of their Afghan guides the following day and he was awestruck and said that some years before a boy had been thrown down that well by his brutal father.'

I stared at Jerwood in amazement.

'Sir Stephen confronted your father about this and he admitted that, in some circumstances, where there was an untimely or violent death and when the place itself was of a certain sort – a sour or tragic place, was how your father put it – then he did, on occasion, see images – silent visions – of the dead.'

Jerwood nodded.

'Yes, Michael,' he said. 'I believe you have inherited that gift – or curse – whichever way you might see it.' He pursed his lips and scowled. 'I am also ashamed to say that Sir Stephen may have asked you to come here in the hope that you would share your father's ability and shed some light on the thing that has clearly been haunting him. It seems that you do.'

'You knew it was Lady Clarendon I saw on the

road, didn't you, sir?' I asked. 'You recognised her from my description?'

Jerwood smiled and sat back in his chair.

'I have not really appreciated what an intelligent young man you are, Michael,' he said. 'Or rather, you are better than intelligent; you are perceptive. Intelligence is a somewhat over-rated virtue. Real intelligence is valuable, of course – but so often people are actually talking about a cleverness, and that is simply a matter of reading and schooling. It is a badge of effort. Perceptiveness is something you are born with, Michael. You can't teach that.'

Jerwood put his long hands together as if in prayer and grew serious once again.

'As I have said,' he continued, 'I have been Sir Stephen's friend since we were school children. I grew up with him and I hope he thought of me as a brother. I know that is how I thought – think – of him.'

Jerwood paused here and shifted in his seat as if the chair had suddenly grown very uncomfortable. I sensed that he was recalling something painful and was struggling to find the words.

'When Sir Stephen and I were at university together I fell in love with a girl, as young men will. But this was a love that I felt was like no other. I loved her with a passion that I had never experienced before – or since.'

'Did you marry her?' I asked.

Jerwood shook his head, of course. This was never going to be a happy tale and I knew him to be a bachelor.

'She married another, Michael,' he said quietly. He picked up his glass and took another sip of brandy. 'She married Sir Stephen.'

I stared wide-eyed. Jerwood had been in love with Lady Clarendon!

'But how . . . ?' I could not understand how Jerwood could have remained friends with a man who had taken his true love from him.

'There was no malice,' he said quietly. 'Stephen loved Margaret and she loved him. He did not take her from me; she chose him freely. I loved him too much to resent it, and her too much to turn my back on her for ever out of some misplaced feeling of rejection.'

He looked at me and saw my wide eyes.

'But still it was hard,' he added.

Neither of us spoke for a few moments and I felt that I was forced to change all my preconceptions about Jerwood, to tear down my image of a cool and logical man and fashion instead an earnest lover and loyal friend.

I was touched that he had entrusted me with this tale. I think I instinctively knew – because my character was not so very different – that Jerwood was a man who did not form attachments easily, and perhaps was therefore all the more open and honest when he did. I was proud beyond words that he thought enough of me, a mere boy with precious little knowledge of the world, to take me into his confidence.

'I think Lady Clarendon fears this place,' I told him.

'Fears this house?' said Jerwood. 'Why would she fear this house? It was her home.'

'There's something else here,' I said.

'In the house?'

'Yes.'

'Have you seen it?' Jerwood asked. 'Is it the ghost of the priest perhaps?'

'No,' I replied. 'I've only seen glimpses. It is a boy – sometimes.'

'Sometimes?' said Jerwood. 'Michael, I want you to tell me everything that has occurred here – everything, mind you, however strange or fanciful it may sound.' He gave me a wry smile. 'However disbelieving you may assume me to be.'

And so I told the lawyer all that I had seen and heard: about the boy in the mirror, the noises, the night visitations, the thing in the priest hole. He listened to it all as gravely and as seriously as though I had been making a perfectly normal witness statement in a court of law. I told him too about Sir Stephen's manic behaviour atop the tower.

When I had finished, he ran his fingers through his hair and looked at me with an expression of amazement and awe.

'The priest hole seems to be at the root of so much of this, Michael. I wonder if the house has always carried that black void inside it like a tumour – if it has always been bad, from the day the place was built.'

I nodded. I felt that too.

'I am so sorry,' said Jerwood quietly. 'Sorry for being party to bringing you here. You shall leave tomorrow with me. I saw Mr Bentley when I was in London and, without telling him much, explained that your visit here might be cut short. They would, of course, be delighted to have you.'

I felt a wave of relief crash over me and I was close to tears.

'I shall square things with Sir Stephen,' said

Jerwood, standing up and patting my shoulder.

'Ah – I almost forgot,' he said, fishing in his pocket and holding out a small blue velvet bag tied with a black cord.

I took the bag and opened it to find a gold pocket watch inside. Prompted by Jerwood, I turned it over and saw my father's name inscribed on it with love from my mother.

'It was your father's,' said Jerwood. 'Mr Bentley asked me to give it to you. Merry Christmas, Michael.'

'Thank you, sir,' I said. 'Thank you.'

CHAPTER EIGHTEEN

There was a tradition at Hawton Mere that the servants and their masters all sat at the Christmas dining table together. It was a fine thing to see that long table laid out its whole length with white linen and silver, candles and holly.

I had the great good fortune to be seated as far away from Sir Stephen as possible, between Mr Jerwood and Hodges. Once Mrs Guston had finished cooking, she and Edith brought the food to the table and sat down opposite us. I realised that there were far more servants working in Hawton Mere than I had previously noticed and they, at least, seemed to know how to enjoy themselves.

And what a feast it was: the Queen herself could not have been partaking of a finer meal. There was a choice of roast turkey or roast goose. The turkey was particularly enormous, the dish taking two maids to bring it in. I had never in my life eaten so well – and rarely since.

I stopped and gazed about me: on all sides of the table conversations were in full flow, and laughter rang out every now and then, the sound bouncing joyfully around the huge room. For the first time since coming to Hawton Mere, I actually enjoyed myself.

I felt I had a small glimpse of the happier place that Hawton Mere must have been in earlier days, for even Sir Stephen looked unusually relaxed and the whole house seemed at ease.

I was, of course, reminded of the Christmases I had spent with my mother: an altogether more meagre affair, but happier for me, by far. Yet, sad though the recollection was, it was not painfully so and I found that I could still enjoy this day – and I was hungry for happiness.

When we had finished our plum pudding, and the dishes had been taken away and we all sat back, full to bursting, Sir Stephen rose from his chair and said that he had some announcements to make.

'I shall not detain you long,' said Sir Stephen, 'but first I want to thank Mrs Guston for providing us with such marvellous food.'

Mrs Guston received warm and enthusiastic applause. She looked exhausted, poor woman, and well she might, having spent the best part of the previous day preparing our feast.

'My sister and I thank you for all the work you have done for us this year and wish you all a very Merry Christmas. We hope that you and your families enjoy the rest of the festivities. You will find the usual tokens of our appreciation on the table in the hall.'

'Merry Christmas to you too, sir,' said Hodges, getting to his feet and raising his glass.

'Merry Christmas!' chimed in the other servants.

Sir Stephen acknowledged the servants and then raised his hand for silence and Hodges sat down again.

'I have another rather important announcement to make,' he continued. 'It concerns young Michael here, whom I hope you have got to know a little during his rather eventful stay at Hawton Mere.'

I felt embarrassed to be the centre of attention, but all faces that now turned to me were smiling broadly – even Jarvis, whose smile, though hardly pleasant, was clearly well meant. I looked at Sir Stephen, wondering, with some trepidation, what he was going to say next.

'I have named Michael as my heir,' he went on. 'When I die, Michael will be the master of Hawton Mere and I think he may prove to be a better one than I have been.'

There were many surprised faces among the servants at this news. Edith looked as though she was about to shriek, her eyes fairly popping from her head. But no one in the room could have looked more shocked than me.

The heir to Hawton Mere? Was this more madness? The staring faces of all about me only increased my sense of embarrassment and I could not hold their gaze. I looked to Jerwood but the lawyer merely smiled back at me.

'I hope when the time comes,' continued Sir Stephen, 'you will treat him with the respect and goodwill you have always shown to me. And so, I would ask you all to raise your glasses and drink a toast to our young friend.'

At this, everyone stood and picked up their glass.

'To Michael,' said Sir Stephen.

'To Michael,' came the response, so loudly and

enthusiastically that I was quite overcome.

Charlotte came round the table and I stood to greet her. She embraced me warmly and so tightly I could feel her long fingernails digging into my back.

'Congratulations, Michael,' she said.

'Congratulations, my boy,' said Jerwood, reaching out to shake my hand, and this action was repeated time and again while I stood in mute incomprehension at this bizarre turn of events. Even Hodges' handshake, which was so vigorous that I felt sure he had broken two of my fingers, was not enough to rouse me from my stupor.

When the excitement of Sir Stephen's announcement died down, the servants cleared the table and the festivities were over. The servants who had family in the village were given leave to visit them. The festive air departed with them.

There is always a melancholy mood that lies in the wake of such festive moments and this was no exception. But my depression was added to by the realisation that, though the servants had generously accepted the idea that I might one day be their master, I still had no wish to adopt that role.

I did not want to spend one more moment in that house than necessary. Ironically, now that Sir

Stephen had made his announcement, the need for me to be at Hawton Mere was satisfied. If this was why he had brought me here, then it was done, and I could go. My fondness for Hodges and the other servants was not enough to make me want to stay. I would never want to live in that house.

I returned to my room and looked at the portrait of Sir Stephen as a boy and tried once again to imagine him running about those rooms, playing with Charlotte, but my thoughts turned instead to his inhuman treatment at the hands of his father. How sad he looked, even then; how fearful.

I hoped that I might marry one day and have children of my own. Why would I bring my family to Hawton Mere? Look what this house had done to Sir Stephen. It had poisoned his childhood and ruined his chance of happiness. It had killed Lady Clarendon.

Lady Clarendon. Poor Lady Clarendon. I looked out of the window and once more I knew before I did so that she would be there. The last bubble of Christmas joy was punctured in an instant by the sight of her ghost. I had felt so relieved when Jerwood had told me that I was going to leave the day after, but what I felt now was guilt.

Edith and Mrs Guston walked out across the

bridge, heading for the village, following the rest of the servants. Lady Clarendon approached them with all the passion and despair with which she had approached our carriage on the night of my arrival, striding towards them with arms outstretched and, though she made no sound, she was clearly calling.

But of course they could not see her. No one could see her. Only me. Mrs Guston and Edith walked on. Lady Clarendon staggered a few paces up the road after them, but eventually stopped and hung her head, her shoulders heaving with sobs. She had grown fainter, as if the effort of trying to contact the servants had exhausted her.

How could I leave that sad creature to haunt the marshes? When I was gone, she would still be here, doomed to walk among the people she once knew, unseen, unheard and unloved. She needed me. There must be some reason why her spirit clung to this place, though she plainly feared it. Who else would discover what it was, if not me?

I ran from my room and along the corridor and down the great staircase, causing Clarence to set up a wild barking and bound after me. I knew that I would not be allowed outside and so I was forced to sneak out. It was not difficult.

'Have you your father's courage?' Sir Stephen had asked me. Time would tell, he said. Now was the time.

I padded out through the courtyard and on to the bridge. Edith and Mrs Guston were only specks in the distance. No one would see me unless they looked out of a window, and that was unlikely – none of the rooms that faced this way were used during the day. Then suddenly I heard footsteps behind me and turned in panic.

But it was Clarence. I tried to shoo him away, but he was having none of it. He had been thoroughly ignored all day and here was his chance for a frolic. We walked out into the snow-covered marsh. But there was no sign of Lady Clarendon's ghost.

The marsh was an inscrutable blanket of whiteness and a mist hung low across the land like immense cobwebs. The moat was thick with ice and the snow was so deep now that the house was the only recognisable feature in view, and even that had been softened by the heavy snow on its roofs and walls.

Clarence bounded ahead, leaping from snowy hummock to snowy hummock, never putting a foot wrong, his tail wagging and sprays of snow dust rising up at every bound, answering patiently every time I blew my Christmas whistle. He would hurtle off into the distance as if chasing some invisible deer and then turn, skidding and slithering, to bound back, his face a picture of joyful abandon.

Every time he came back to me I braced myself, expecting him to leap up at me and knock me flat on my back, but seconds before crashing into me, he would swerve with practised agility and avoid me entirely, running rings round me and jumping in the air like a puppy, so pleased was he with himself.

After he had done this six or seven times and I had laughed and patted him warmly, he ran round me as he had done all the other times but, almost in mid-jump, he came to a halt and stared off into the distance.

'What is it, boy?' I said, following his gaze and seeing nothing there but empty snow.

In response, the hair on his back began to stand on end and he dropped his head, sniffing the air. Then he began to growl.

'Clarence, you silly dog,' I said. 'There's nothing there.'

But when I looked up again, there was Lady Clarendon, pale as the surrounding snow.

Clarence edged forward, sniffing and growling. I thought that he might recognise his former mistress, though he could only have been a puppy then, and calm himself, but I quickly realised that he did not see her at all – he merely sensed something that had raised his hackles. He walked straight through her, his grey form sliding through Lady Clarendon's ghost as though he had stepped through a sheet of ice.

The effect of this encounter on the poor dog was profound, for he whimpered and then bounded away, barking forlornly as he went.

I wanted to run too, like Clarence, back to the house and back to the living. I felt a wave of sadness and despair seep towards me through the chill air as Lady Clarendon held out her hand and beckoned me, then walked over to the moat. I followed her and we stopped at the place where I had fallen in and almost drowned. Lady Clarendon looked at me and pointed up, across the moat.

I saw the balcony with the door above us. The thick walls sparkled with frost and icicles hung from beneath. But I already knew that she had fallen from the balcony.

Then, to my astonishment, I saw another Lady Clarendon appear above the low parapet – the lovely, healthy and living Lady Clarendon of the portrait. I realised straight away that I was about to witness her death. But why?

The living Lady Clarendon leaned forward on the balcony, her face a picture of joy. The cold air gave her cheeks a rosy glow and though this glimpse of the past, like the ghost herself, was silent, I could tell that Lady Clarendon was calling out across the marshes, as if announcing great news to the world.

But as she raised high her arms, something rushed at her – a dark shape that surged forward from the shadows of the room behind her. With horrible suddenness, Lady Clarendon was toppled from the balcony. I saw nothing of her attacker save for the pale hands that pushed her.

The body seemed to take an age to hit the ice but it was terrible when it did. The silence was worse somehow. She disappeared from sight, leaving a gaping black wound in the frozen surface. More horrible still, she floated up, her wide-eyed, pitiful face just visible through the translucent ice.

The bubbles had long since ceased to emerge from her open mouth when Sir Stephen and Hodges came silently running over the bridge. Pausing beside us only long enough to let out a

long silent animal moan, Sir Stephen leapt headlong into the moat, with Hodges mouthing his
name.

Jerwood arrived as the flailing Sir Stephen
managed to drag the body of his wife to the side.
He allowed himself to be pulled out by Jerwood
while Hodges carried the lifeless form of Lady
Clarendon back to the house.

I stood and watched as Jerwood helped his old
friend to follow behind, Sir Stephen bellowing his
wife's name and screaming with despair.

I looked back to the ghost of Lady Clarendon,
but she was gone. Then, so too was the world she
had shown me. Jerwood, Sir Stephen, Hodges, the
body of poor Lady Clarendon: all gone. I was alone
again.

CHAPTER NINETEEN

I had to speak to Jerwood and tell him what I had seen. He alone of all the people I knew might believe me and know best what to do to apprehend the murderer.

For that was why Lady Clarendon haunted this place. It was not simply that she had had a troubled life; it was that her life had been cruelly taken from her and made to look like suicide. There was a wrong to be righted: a murderer to be unmasked.

And I was in no doubt who that murderer must be. Though I had not seen the attacker, I had seen

Sir Stephen enough times to feel certain he alone was capable of such a thing. He was given to bouts of wild – even violent – behaviour, and now I was sure that it was guilt that was adding to the torments of his mind. I remembered him urging me to leap from the tower and thought of poor Lady Clarendon tumbling into that moat.

I knew that Jerwood was with Sir Stephen in Sir Stephen's study. I would have preferred to wait until I could find Jerwood alone but I could not keep this to myself for a moment longer. Perhaps, I thought, it would be better to confront him in front of his old friend and see what happened.

I ran into the house, ignoring the barking of Clarence in the courtyard. I ran up the stairs and through the door that led to the tower. I ran up the twisting spiral staircase, round and round, until I arrived dizzy and out of breath at the study door, which I opened without knocking.

Having burst in so dramatically, I was taken aback to find that the study was empty. I ran up the stairs to the roof of the tower, but that too was deserted. I climbed back down and returned to the main part of the house, trying to think where Jerwood might be.

I decided that I would head to the kitchen. At

least then I might find Hodges, who would surely know what to do. But I had barely set out on my way down the passageway when I noticed that the door to Lady Clarendon's room was ajar. I peered inside and saw Charlotte standing by the door leading to the balcony.

'I'm sorry,' I said and made to leave.

'Michael,' she said, turning. 'What can I do for you?'

'I was looking for Mr Jerwood,' I replied.

Charlotte smiled. She tapped at the door frame with her long fingernails. She was wearing a black velvet dress that made her pale skin look as white as the winter sky behind her. I wondered what she was doing in that room, but I had more immediate concerns.

'Whatever's the matter, Michael?' she asked. 'You look upset. Can I help?'

'Not really,' I said. 'It's something that concerns Sir Stephen.'

'Then it concerns me,' she said. 'What is it?'

'I'm sorry, ma'am. But I think I want to speak to Mr Jerwood first.'

'I am Sir Stephen's sister, Michael,' said Charlotte. 'Surely anything you have to say about my brother, you can say to me?'

I didn't know what to reply. I felt very strongly that it was Jerwood who should first receive this news, but there was no polite way to tell her this.

'Won't you join me on the balcony?' she said, stepping out through the door. I had no desire to go out on to that place, knowing what had happened there, but I edged towards it nonetheless.

'I really must find Mr Jerwood,' I said again. I did not want to be openly rude to Charlotte but I knew that her instinct would be to excuse and protect her brother and so there seemed little point in discussing my feelings with her.

'Oh nonsense, Michael,' she said. 'I'm sure Mr Jerwood can wait – whatever this mysterious business you have with him is. Come along. The view is marvellous.'

I stood reluctantly in the doorway but Charlotte grabbed my arm and pulled me on to the balcony to stand alongside her. She was right: the view was indeed marvellous. So long as I did not look down.

Charlotte proceeded to point out various landmarks with her long fingers and it was then that I saw it, and all at once the truth dazzled in my eyes.

For something green twinkled in the sunlight – and in my memory.

'It was you!' I gasped. I had seen that same green

sparkle blinking brightly on the hand that had pushed Lady Clarendon. Sir Stephen wore no jewellery at all. It had not been his hand I saw. It had been Charlotte's.

'I beg your pardon, Michael,' she said.

'Poor Lady Clarendon,' I said, noticing that Charlotte had now moved behind me, blocking the exit from the balcony. 'She didn't kill herself. You murdered her.'

Charlotte frowned and squinted at me as if she were a scientist presented with a curious new bug. A flurry of expressions flickered across her face. She took a step towards me and I backed away, stumbling. Charlotte chuckled like a little girl.

'What an odd creature you are, Michael. Now why would you think such a thing?' She gave me a mischievous, though contemptuous, look. 'This is her room,' she said. 'Stephen keeps it as a shrine. Isn't that ridiculous? It is just as it was that day she jumped.'

'She didn't jump,' I said. 'You pushed her. Why?' I looked backwards for a moment, and saw a dizzying glimpse of the frozen moat below. 'Why would you kill your brother's wife?'

Charlotte sighed and turned her back to me.

'Because she was weak, Michael,' she said as if she

found the question infuriating. 'I cannot abide weakness. Stephen is weak – weak-minded – but he is my brother and what am I to do? I have looked after him as best as I could, but Hawton Mere must be protected. This house comes first, Michael. Always. If you truly belonged here, you would understand.'

'You've helped to make him like that!' I said.

Charlotte stared back at me from the doorway and then grinned. She picked up something I couldn't see from a dressing table just inside the room.

'Margaret was a silly woman,' she said after a pause. 'Stephen would insist on marrying her, but she was not good enough for him. She was not good enough for Hawton Mere. She was pretty and kind, of course, but strength is what this house needs. My father understood that.'

Charlotte looked towards me again and sighed.

'What sort of a child would they have had together, Michael? To think that if it had been a boy it would inherit this house – this house I have given my life to. No! She drove me to it. She was to blame, not I.'

'You mean she was going to have a child?' I cried. I remembered the joyful expression on the living

Lady Clarendon's face before she was pushed. 'What kind of monster are you?'

I regretted the harshness of my tone, as Charlotte turned to me and I saw a large pair of scissors gripped tightly in her hand.

'But how is it that you have discovered this?' she said. 'Who has filled your head with this nonsense? Hodges, no doubt!' Charlotte came closer, examining my face. There was nothing to be gained now by lying to her.

'It was Lady Clarendon herself,' I said. 'Her spirit took me back in time. I saw you push her from the balcony with my own eyes.'

Charlotte stared at me for a moment, taking in what I had told her. Then she collapsed into laughter. But it was a dry and mirthless laughter.

'Listen to yourself, you silly, silly boy,' she said.

'But you have already admitted it's true!'

'Have I? If I have it is only to you. And you already have rather a reputation for fantasy, do you not? In any case, I fear you may be about to have another unfortunate accident.'

I turned away, unable to bear looking at her. She moved closer and her dress made a swish I now recognised as the whispering sound I heard behind me that day in the snow.

'You pushed me into the moat!'

'But Michael,' said Charlotte with a smile, 'you fell in the moat. It was an accident. Don't you remember?'

'I do remember,' I said. 'I remember that whispering sound and I remember feeling something on my back just before I slipped. And you changed your dress. You changed your dress because it was wet from the snow.'

Charlotte sighed.

'Did you seriously think that I would stand idly by and watch you – you! – inherit Hawton Mere? I'll die first!'

'It's not for you to say!' I shouted. 'Sir Stephen has –'

'Pah!' snorted Charlotte. 'Stephen is a madman and there are a hundred witnesses to the fact.'

'He was locked up in that terrible place by your father. It's no wonder,' I said.

Charlotte giggled. 'Oh, you know about that, do you?'

She smiled coquettishly, twirling the scissors as if they were a fan. I glanced past her to the door across the room. It was still slightly open. Perhaps I might reach it if I could just get past Charlotte. But I would have to be fast.

'Shall I tell you a secret?' she whispered. I made no reply. 'It wasn't Stephen who did that to my father's study . . .' She edged a little closer. 'It was me.'

'What?' I said. 'So . . . So Sir Stephen owned up to save you from a thrashing?'

'Ironic, isn't it?' she said. 'The one and only time he had the nerve to stand up to Father and he hadn't actually done anything wrong. Even Father would have been impressed had he known. It was Stephen's first and last act of bravery.'

I saw my chance and rushed at Charlotte, barging past her into the room and running to the door and pulling it open. To my horror, standing in the doorway was Sir Stephen, his dark glasses black against his ashen face, the jet buttons on his waistcoat twinkling like dying stars.

'Maybe not my last, Charlotte,' he said, looking past me to his sister.

'Stephen,' said Charlotte, with a sugary lightness in her voice that was as alarming as the malevolence that had preceded it. 'How long have you been standing there?'

'So you killed her, Charlotte?' Sir Stephen said quietly, his face and voice devoid of expression. 'You murdered Margaret?'

'But Stephen, surely you didn't believe that nonsense. I was just humouring Michael,' she said, her tone switching to one of wounded innocence. 'Do you really think me capable of murder?'

'I believe you would do anything for this house,' Sir Stephen replied.

Charlotte faltered a little in the face of Sir Stephen's coldness, but she walked towards him, arms outstretched.

'You are tired, brother . . .' she began.

'Enough!' said Sir Stephen, pushing her away, and refusing to even look at her face. He walked instead towards me and clasped both hands round my shoulders, smiling sadly.

'Michael,' he said, 'go and fetch Mr Jerwood. He is with –'

But before he could finish these words, he gasped, looked at me with an expression of bafflement, then dropped to my feet to reveal Charlotte standing behind him holding the scissors, crimson smears on their silver blades.

I fell to my haunches and tried to pick Sir Stephen up, but he made no sound. Blood was oozing from a wound in his back and, when I turned him over, more blood trickled from between his lips. I placed my ear beside his mouth and there was no sound, no breath.

'He's dead!' I said, looking at Charlotte and seeing the scissors whirl towards me in a wide arc. I managed to move just in time to save my eye as the blades flashed past my face.

I struck out wildly, but with enough force to knock the scissors from Charlotte's hand and send them clattering across the floor. I scrambled backwards but Charlotte lurched with surprising speed and startling strength. She grasped me round the throat and began to choke me. I tried to prise away her arms but to no avail; she held me like a vice.

As we struggled round the room, my flailing arm caught a lamp on the table and sent it to the floor, where the oil spilled across the carpet, igniting as it did so and catching the edge of the great damask curtains.

The fire seemed to take hold in every surface of the room instantaneously. No sooner had it begun than it encircled us entirely. Charlotte did not appear to notice, so crazed was she now. With all my remaining strength I struck her in the face as hard as I could.

Charlotte let go of me and staggered back. The flames were alive, rearing up here and there like burning stallions, kicking out with fiery hooves.

But there was a path between the flames and I ran through, shielding my face against the heat, and managed to reach the door leading to the hallway beyond. Charlotte tried to follow me, but the waves of fire crashed back like the Red Sea over Pharaoh.

She screamed after me, more in fury than in fear. I turned to see her twisted, raging hate-filled face and thought that were there any justice, these flames would be only a taste of those yet to come.

I stepped out of the burning room and into the passageway, shocked to see that the fire was already escaping and moving with a supernatural energy, sizzling in the ceiling above my head and visible between the floorboards at my feet. The plaster-work was cracking and falling. Smoke was seeping through. I was about to run, when I was brought to a halt by what I saw ahead.

Standing some ten feet away, with his back to me and his head bowed, was a boy about my own age – though his clothes were somewhat old-fashioned.

I knew in an instant that this was the boy I had seen in the mirror. He was muttering to himself, clenching and unclenching his fists. Even from the back I could sense his rage. Then he turned to face me.

I had seen much at Hawton Mere to chill my

blood, but nothing – nothing! – had prepared me for the sight I now beheld. The boy turned to face me, but the face he showed had no eyes or nose or any feature at all save a mouth – a mouth that now opened like a vicious wound to let out a cry that seemed to shatter the very air about us. It was a cry that summoned up a world of anger and pain in one terrifying sound.

He ran towards me and I swear that my heart stopped there and then and only beat again when he raced past, uninterested in me. I turned to see his form shift this way and that: a cockroach-spider-lizard thing, galloping towards its prey on bristled legs. Through the shimmering heat haze I saw Charlotte.

The thing stood before her in the fire glow. It was a boy once again: the boy whose brooding, violent spirit was such a part of this house. And I saw that she, like me, could now clearly recognise him for who he was.

He was not a ghost at all. Or, at least, he was not the ghost of a deceased person. He was the ghost of a child whose life had been so damaged that the pain of it had manifested itself as this strange and terrifying entity. It was Sir Stephen as a boy.

When Charlotte saw the boy, her face changed to

one of terror. She recognised, as did I, the intensity of hatred and bitterness in that awful face. Her cruelty and obsession had spawned this creature the day she let her brother take the blame and saw him locked in the priest hole. Sir Stephen had been haunted by himself all those years. Now the demon that had tormented him had come for her.

Fiery snakes were hissing at my head and feet, slithering along the passageway and threatening to cut off my escape if I did not move quickly. But just as I began to run, a beam fell from the ceiling and blocked my way. The heat from the flames hurt my eyes.

I fumbled inside my pocket and blew the whistle. There was no sound to take comfort in, but still I hoped that somewhere it would be heard and help might come.

Smoke plumed up and stung my throat. The ceiling collapsed behind me. The air around me was becoming unbearably hot, and my breaths became shallower and shallower.

I could see very little now, and I must confess I thought that this might be where my story would end. But then Hodges and Jerwood came running towards me, Clarence barking at their heels.

Hodges cleared the burning timber away with

total disregard for his own safety.

'Michael!' shouted Jerwood as they reached me. 'What has happened here? Where is Sir Stephen?'

'He's back there . . . in Lady Clarendon's bedroom . . . So is Miss Charlotte,' I began, coughing at the smoke that coiled about us.

Hodges leapt forward and began knocking aside the burning rafters with his bare hands, struggling against all reasonable odds to break through, despite his very clothes catching alight as he did so. The fire reared up and attacked him, burning his hair.

Jerwood tried to pull him back but Hodges turned in such a rage of passion that I thought he would strike Jerwood down, before shrugging the lawyer away and returning to his efforts. This was the loyalty that Sir Stephen had so admired in my father. But was another brave man to die out of loyalty to Sir Stephen?

'Mr Hodges!' I cried tearfully, grabbing hold of him and turning his face towards mine. 'Don't! Oh please don't! He's dead. Sir Stephen's already dead! And you'll die too if you go in there!'

'But what about Miss Charlotte?' he shouted.

'It was she who killed Sir Stephen,' I gasped. 'And she murdered Lady Clarendon too.' Hodges and

Jerwood exchanged astonished glances. 'It's true!' Another part of the ceiling crashed down.

'You'll never reach her, Hodges!' shouted Jerwood.

I had imbibed so much smoke during this speech that I could now barely breathe, choking as Hodges stood for a moment weighing my words. After a second or two, he nodded.

'For God's sake, let's get out of here!' shouted Jerwood, and this time Hodges made no resistance.

Part of the house seemed to collapse at our every footfall. The sound of the conflagration was deafening and behind it all there was that awful groaning, moaning, growling sound of despair shaking the house to its very foundations.

We staggered, coughing and choking, out into the courtyard, and we each helped the others to run across the bridge and out into the safety of the marsh. Hodges' clothes were still smouldering in places, giving him a wild air as he stood and looked back towards the house.

Flames were leaping from the roof and from the window, and the yellow and red of its light flickered and danced upon the snow and the ice of the moat. I found myself irresistibly drawn to the balcony, and Hodges and Jerwood followed.

The light of day was fading and the eerie

glimmer of twilight washed the scene. Rose-red clouds billowed above us. We stood by the moat, looking up at the blazing room.

But Charlotte was not dead yet. She appeared at the balcony, screaming in terror. I could see something behind her, black in front of the tumult of flames. It was less boy now and more monkey, more demon or imp, and it hopped this way and that in triumph until Charlotte, in her desperation to escape it and the flames, climbed on to the parapet, ripping her burning dress from her body, and leapt into the frozen moat in nothing but her white shift.

To his great credit, Hodges jumped into the icy moat to try to save her, but it seemed to take her under and Hodges could not find her in the thick, murky water. Jerwood and I helped to pull him out and, as we ushered him away, Charlotte's body floated up from the depths and rested, just as Lady Clarendon's had, below the thick ice, the light of the fire washing over her frozen and distorted features.

I glanced back once, as we walked to the bridge, and saw the ghost of Lady Clarendon at the edge of the fire glow. She stood at the moat's edge, staring down at Charlotte's body. She turned to look at me briefly and then, walking backwards, disappeared into the darkness, not merely to be hidden by it, but to be subsumed by it, engulfed in it. She simply became part of the blackness. She was gone now, I supposed, never to return.

CHAPTER TWENTY

The events I have described are all now long past, not that they have ever faded in their intensity. They are as potent in my mind now as they ever were. I wish to God I could have made them fade. I wish to God I could rid my dreams of their awful shapes.

Funerals and weddings tend to conjure up visions of other funerals and weddings, and Charlotte and Sir Stephen's ceremony inevitably made me recollect that poorly attended and dismal funeral of my dear mother, though it seemed a lifetime ago and was a very different sort of affair.

We three – Jerwood, Hodges and I – had agreed that the best we could do in the circumstances was to say that it had been what it appeared to be: a terrible accident. We did not even tell Mrs Guston or Edith or the Bentleys. What good would it have done?

Sir Stephen's rank ensured that the service at Ely cathedral was a grand and spectacular occasion. The massive and rather grotesque marble monument to Sir Stephen and Charlotte looms over visitors there to this day, a talking point for guides, who tell the tragic story of how brother and sister died together and lie together for all eternity. It is a very moving tale they say, when told well.

Sir Stephen's neighbours turned out in abundance, expensively dressed in black like a flock of carrion crows. The womenfolk cried and swooned and sobbed behind handkerchiefs and fans, but I did not believe their grief. Those who had gossiped about Sir Stephen while he lived now hoped to profit by his death.

I stood apart with Jerwood and with Hodges, whose hands and face still bore the shiny pink scars of his wild efforts to reach Sir Stephen in the fire. We had forged a bond now. Any suspicion which might have fallen upon me as the inheritor of Sir Stephen's wealth was cleared by the presence of Jerwood, whose reputation as an honest man was second to none.

That said, the neighbours were very happy to speculate, of course, and I could see small groups whispering darkly whenever I turned round. But I could not have cared less, though I must confess I gained some pleasure from the fact that all their cries and wailing were for naught. Sir Stephen had chosen to remember none of them in his will.

Hawton Mere was reduced to a blackened, crumbling ruin by the fire and all the paintings and accumulated treasures of its ancient family were likewise destroyed.

But Sir Stephen's wealth did not solely reside in the stones of Hawton Mere – far from it. Sir Stephen owned land for miles about and much property besides. He was a shareholder in many businesses, both here and abroad. It was Jerwood's job as his lawyer and friend to make sense of this vast fortune and distribute it in accordance with Sir Stephen's wishes. The distribution was simple at least. With Charlotte dead, the fortune was all to be directed to one person: the author of this tale.

When Jerwood explained that I was the sole heir to the whole of Sir Stephen's estate, I was at first shocked and then resentful. I did not want this money. I had done nothing to deserve it and I did not want the association with all the pain and misery of that place and that family. In particular, I did not want any link with Charlotte.

But Jerwood, in his kind way, and then subsequently the kindly Bentleys both convinced me that it was Sir Stephen's will and I should not let pride check this great opportunity in my life.

Initially reluctant, I came to see the sense of what they said and eventually assented. Jerwood explained that I did not actually need to be involved in any of Sir Stephen's business dealings. He had people in place to manage all those matters. When I had come to an age when I might take an interest in those affairs, then an opening could certainly be found for me. In the meantime, I was to continue with my education. The capital would be held in a trust for me and Jerwood would administer to my day-to-day needs.

Jerwood did have one suggestion though, one to which I was quick to agree. He suggested that it might be appropriate to bestow a sum of money upon each of the servants from Hawton Mere, giving a special sum to Hodges for his loyalty to Sir Stephen over the years.

Jerwood had already seen to it that the servants had gained employment elsewhere and was tireless in his endeavours to ensure that all those connected with the house were looked after. It was almost as if he took on the burdens of Sir Stephen with an enthusiasm – as though by so doing it brought him closer to his dear departed friend.

All this done, I returned to my former school – and how oddly normal that now seemed – and to a world that appeared childish after the events at Hawton Mere. I found that the boys who had been offhand when I had arrived now looked diminished in size and importance.

Perhaps because I paid them no heed, and perhaps because I now gave off an aura that spoke of my trials and adventures, some of the boys sought me out and I began, in a hesitating fashion at first, to form friendships for the first time for many years.

I was now a good and enthusiastic scholar. The teachers encouraged me to ever higher achievements, until one day I stood on the steps of my college in Cambridge, unable for a moment to quite believe my good fortune.

I will not bore you with tales of my university life, of the studies I undertook, of the friends I made or of the girl I met and loved and who, when she took her leave of me one sunny day beside the Cam, drove me to take to the continent on a kind of Grand Tour.

I strode about the Alps in melancholy isolation, taunting death on more than one occasion with my reckless disregard for the weather or terrain – a wanderer above the clouds.

But wherever I roamed I could not rid myself of Hawton Mere. For many months, on many a night, I would have the same repeating dream that I was lost somewhere, surrounded by fog and mist, unable to discern any features at all.

I would walk and walk with no clear direction, but always I would find myself in the same place: at the moat's edge at Hawton Mere, the water frozen all about.

Looking down I would see a shape beneath the ice, a form becoming more distinct as I watched, until I saw with mounting horror that it was the staring face of Charlotte, fixing me with a look of murderous hatred. The ice above her head would crack and I would wake bathed in cold sweat and shivering as though I really had been standing there.

I wandered the great cities of Europe, and saw

wondrous works of art and architecture. I wrote poetry of a particularly gloomy nature. But whatever solace I sought from nature or art, it was not forthcoming, and I began to yearn for the familiar voices of England.

I knew that if I was to leave Hawton Mere behind me, I had to face my fear, not try to hide.

CHAPTER TWENTY-ONE

I was in Sicily when I made the decision to return and found passage aboard a ship bound for Bristol. I never got on so well with anyone during all my travels as I did with Captain Mayhew, and by the time we docked in England we knew all there was to know about each other.

A seafaring man will usually trump a landlubber when it comes to the telling of tales, but he was forced to admit that my experiences made his life seem tame in comparison. He was fascinated and never once disputed a single thing I said, however extraordinary it must have sounded, however unbelievable.

By the time we had reached Bristol we were firm friends and I vowed to stay in contact with him through his shipping office and we both hoped that we might meet again some day.

I sent a telegram to the Bentleys and to Jerwood as soon as I arrived and then took the locomotive to London. The Bentleys met me at the station and could not have been more pleased had I been their own dearest son returning; and, in truth, they seemed like family to me now.

'You are so thin!' shrieked Mrs Bentley as she embraced me. 'You're not looking after yourself, Michael.'

'I am quite well, Mrs Bentley,' I said. 'Honestly.'

'Leave the boy be, Sybil,' said Mr Bentley, straightening my coat and dusting the sleeves with his hand. 'Don't fuss, don't fuss.'

We took a cab to their house in Highgate and I told them something – but by no means all – of my adventures, and they listened in rapt attention, punctuating the tale with occasional gasps of amazement.

Their house was just as I remembered it. I had spent many days here over the years. The Bentleys had shown me such kindness. If I could have stayed anywhere, I would have stayed there. They had kept a room for me as they promised they would, and after an enormous dinner and a chance to hear the Bentleys' news, I slept very soundly indeed.

The following day I took a cab to Lincoln's Inn Fields to see Jerwood. The lawyer and I had a different relationship than I had with the Bentleys, but in some ways it was closer still for our shared experiences at Hawton Mere.

He greeted me at the door like an old friend and neither of us could speak for some moments. I knew that I had changed considerably in my time away, but he did not look a day older and was his usual, impeccably dressed self. But he did have one surprise for me.

I entered Jerwood's study to find Hodges standing before me. My joy at seeing that fine fellow was tempered by the fact that the whole history of Hawton Mere seemed to be written in his face – quite literally so, with the burns he suffered in the fire still visible. But oh, how pleased I was to see him. He grabbed me by both arms and lifted me clean off the floor.

'Master Michael!' he said. 'Thank God you've come back safe and sound.'

'Well said,' added Jerwood, picking up a decanter of port and pouring three glasses.

Hodges told us of his current employer, who sounded like a thoroughly decent sort, and of Mrs Guston and Edith, who held posts in the same house. Even Jarvis, the garrulous coach driver, was there.

'Edith asked me to send her special best wishes,' he said with a wink. I blushed a little and Jerwood seemed to enjoy this enormously.

On a sadder note, Hodges told me of the death of poor old Clarence. I reached into my pocket and brought out the whistle Hodges had made me that Christmas. I had carried it with me on all my travels and I told him it had brought me much comfort in my difficulties. He was very touched.

The events at Hawton Mere were never directly spoken of by us. The subject was never prohibited by anyone, it was merely an understanding among the three of us. None of us wanted, it seemed, to revisit that place, even in words.

But though I willingly complied for friendship's sake, I had long before decided that the only way I would be free of those memories was to confront them. I decided that I would, one last time, look on the fallen remnants of Hawton Mere. The house and the things that had taken place there were never far from the forefront of my mind and, worse, they still came unbidden to my sleeping thoughts.

I imagined that if I was to go to Hawton Mere, to see it as a ruin and nothing more, that this might in some degree serve as an exorcism. I was a child no longer. I had faced many dangers since that last day at Hawton Mere. I felt that I could stare it in its shattered face and say, 'Be gone!'

I did not tell the Bentleys or Jerwood where I was bound, though Jerwood, I am sure, had strong suspicions. I caught the train to Ely and hired a horse and rode through those flatlands with a quickening heart. I spurred the horse on and we careered down those lanes as if the devil was at our tail. Then, all at once, we were at the track that led to Hawton Mere, and I kicked the horse on one more time.

I could sense the unwillingness of the beast to venture further. I could sense the fear in his great flanks and see the nervous twitching in his ears. I could feel his dread and he could no doubt sense mine.

If anything, the house looked more daunting as a ruin than it had as a complete house, with its crippled roof, its shattered walls and skull-like empty window sockets. It was as malevolent as a dead house as it had been as a living one. More so perhaps.

The land all about it now seemed utterly poisoned, as if the sickness of the house had leeched out into the surroundings. The moat looked filled with tar, or worse, to be some kind of void – the blackness of some bottomless chasm.

I encouraged my reluctant horse to cross the bridge and it was a mark of its trust in me that it so successfully buried its fear and did as I asked.

The courtyard beyond the gatehouse was almost unrecognisable. It had once been contained by the buildings around it, but half of these had tumbled to the ground. Sir Stephen's tower remained, but only as a severely wounded survivor, the back of it having collapsed entirely. I dismounted and tied my horse to a post, where it looked at me with a wide-eyed entreaty to make my stay a brief one. I smiled and patted its neck and whispered assurances that I would not be long.

It was as I spoke to him thus that I beheld, from the corner of my eye, a sudden movement some way off, beyond the broken tower. It was a fleeting glimpse and no more and I quickly began to wonder if I had imagined it when a flock of pigeons took flight from the roof and I smiled to myself at my own childish jitters.

But it had not been a pigeon I had seen. Looking towards the back of the tower, I saw the movement again and realised that there was someone there, moving away from the main part of Hawton Mere, towards the end of the island on which it stood.

I started to follow, my view forever limited by fallen masonry or branches, and as I did so I began to have sorry presentiments about who exactly it was.

I had assumed that with Charlotte's death, all ghostly activity would cease at Hawton Mere. It seemed not just lifeless, but lacking in all activity, all energy of any kind. I had hoped that Lady Clarendon was reunited with Sir Stephen and at peace now – or if not at peace, then at least at rest.

But as I finally turned a corner I could see full well that about thirty feet away was Lady Clarendon's ghost, her back turned to me, looking out in grim contemplation of the black waters of the moat.

'Lady Clarendon,' I said. 'It's me, Michael.'

She did not move.

'Lady Clarendon,' I repeated.

Again she made no move, but stood there pale and still. I walked towards her with mounting unease, for I wondered what new tragedy had entrapped her once again and forced her to haunt these ruins.

When I was a few feet away, I called her name again. This time she seemed to hear, and slowly turned around. Her wet hair hung across her face, but as she raised her head I saw that it was not Lady Clarendon at all, but someone else – someone I recognised all too well, despite the burns that disfigured her face. It was Charlotte.

As I recoiled in horror, her face shone with a light of pure evil. Her eyes that had been so bright in life were now white marbles, as if the fire had licked all colour from them. She was like some spider who had waited for this moment, and now the moment came she struck, lurching forward at terrifying speed. I ran as fast as my legs would take me to my horse, untying it with shaking hands and mounting just as Charlotte floated into the wrecked courtyard, her head to one side as if study-ing something peculiar – and then she rushed towards me.

The horse needed little encouragement to bolt and it launched itself through the gatehouse with such enthusiasm that I think it would have cleared the moat without the benefit of a bridge. We galloped down that road away from Hawton Mere and I made no move to turn my head and look back. I would never look at that place again.

I decided in that instant that I would quit this country.

EPILOGUE

So now I sit, pen in hand, about to lay that pen down for good, having told my story to the fullest of my abilities. As I began, so I shall finish: if you have read these words and still cannot find yourself to consider the narrative anything more than the fevered imaginings of a young man who has read too many novels of a Gothic bent, then I can say no more than to assure you once again that I have said nothing but the truth on every line.

I telegraphed Captain Mayhew when I returned to London and told him that I wished to sail with him wherever he was bound. His response was that he would be delighted to have me and that he was to sail to Argentina in a week's time.

My parting with Jerwood was a solemn affair. I did not tell him about my visit to Hawton Mere and Charlotte's ghost. I saw no need to burden him further.

The Bentleys were distraught of course. Mr Bentley was so upset I do not think I saw him twitch once – not even the merest spasm. Mrs Bentley seemed intent on making my departure impossible by breaking every bone in my body with her bear-like embraces. She assured me that the entire population of that part of the world were either cannibals or Catholics.

'All will be well,' said Bentley quietly as we stood together on the platform. 'All will be well.'

'I hope so, Mr Bentley,' I said, and boarded the train.

So here I am in my hotel room in Bristol. Tomorrow I join Mayhew's ship and sail for Buenos Aires. From there I will head inland. I have heard that there are great opportunities in that country and I relish the chance to lose myself in a foreign land once more.

The voyage cannot come quickly enough, for though I have seen nothing to speak of, I have felt pursued ever since I saw the spectre of Charlotte at the ruins of Hawton Mere. Some of the tension I felt in that house has returned and I seem to start at every floorboard creak. I am like a frightened child once more.

But what is that? Something comes, I can sense it. The wind outside has dropped and there is a deathly hush about the place. I am in a low and lively quarter of the port and yet an uncanny silence has descended upon the area.

Yet there is a whispering. No – not a whisper: a dry slither, like the scales of a snake. And now there is a tapping. It was light at first, but is getting stronger. *Tap. Tap. Tap, tap, tap.* It is on the window-pane on the other side of the heavy curtain of the room I am renting. *Tap, tap, tap.* I have heard that sound before.

Looking at the curtain in front of me, I am reminded of that tapestry curtain at Hawton Mere that I pulled aside to reveal the portrait of Lady Clarendon, or the bedroom curtain that concealed her ghost on the moat's edge. What does *this* curtain conceal? I think I know. Oh God, I think I know.

The only way to be certain is to lay down my pen and open it.

READ ON FOR CHRIS PRIESTLEY'S GUIDE TO HORROR:

💀 Things that go bump in the night — why we love Horror

💀 Chris Priestley's favourite spinechillers

💀 Creative tips for writing creepy stories

💀 A conversation with the author

THINGS THAT GO BUMP IN THE NIGHT — WHY WE LOVE HORROR

I have a suspicion that horror is one of the oldest genres in fiction. Just as I can imagine our hunter-gatherer forebears coming home and telling a funny story, I can easily see, as night fell and the clan was gathered around the fire, that scary tales were told.

Horror has always been part of myth and religion. If religion is an attempt to make sense of the world, then maybe horror is an acceptance that we cannot know everything – that there will always be areas of impenetrable darkness.

Certainly folk tales and fairy stories often contained large doses of horror. Anyone concerned about the effect of horror on the young should go and have a look at any of the pre-Disneyfied stories of the Brothers Grimm.

I deliberately began *Uncle Montague's Tales of Terror* with a walk through a wood, because I wanted to make use of that fairytale opening. The stories themselves are set not so much in the real Victorian or Edwardian era, but in the world of Victorian and Edwardian ghost stories.

Some genres seem like literary constructs:

completely a product of writing. But horror, like love, is there in the world. I don't mean that vampires or zombies are there, but the dread that produces these nightmares certainly is. Fear is ever present.

But whilst it is obvious why people want to read love stories, it is less clear why people want to frighten themselves unnecessarily, whether through books, movies or hurling themselves into a ravine with a length of elastic attached to their ankles.

We seem to enjoy scaring ourselves. Maybe we want to test ourselves; to see how we would cope with real fear. Of course, this is utterly spurious. We know we aren't really going to hit the ground. We know it's only a story.

But even so. Maybe we just need to push that button every now and then to make sure it still works. Maybe through horror stories we get a chance to leap headlong into the dark – in the comforting knowledge that we have elastic tied to our ankles.

CHRIS PRIESTLEY'S FAVOURITE SPINECHILLERS

Any list of favourite books is, by nature, temporary. But these are a few I think will always stay with me.

Tales of Mystery and Imagination by Edgar Allan Poe

I remember being quite shocked by Poe when I first read these stories. I had seen the Roger Corman adaptation of several of them, but they did not prepare me for the weirdness of the actual tales. This is bizarre, hallucinogenic horror that, despite the florid language, seems very modern in its focus on the psychology of its characters – on their obsessions, anxieties and very dark desires.

The Haunting of Hill House by Shirley Jackson

I didn't read The Haunting of Hill House until quite recently. The 1963 movie of the book has always been a favourite of mine, but Shirley Jackson's book is far more complex than the movie and is superbly written. Both The Haunting and Poe's The Fall of the House of Usher were influences on my last book, The Dead of Winter.

Ghost Stories of an Antiquary by M. R. James

Like Shirley Jackson, I came to M. R. James via

adaptations. His work was filmed in the 1970s by Lawrence Gordon Clark for the BBC's A *Ghost Story for Christmas*. The tales are stranger and darker than you might think if you know them only by their cosy 'traditional ghost story' reputation. 'A Warning to the Curious' is one of his best and could almost stand as a theme for a lot of his work.

I *am Legend* by Richard Matheson

Is this a horror book or a sci-fi book? Actually, it's neither and both. The writing is taut and though the scenario is fantastic (a man holding out against the mass victims of a kind of plague of vampirism) it is never less than horribly believable. Tense and nerve-jangling to the very end.

The Dunwich Horror by H. P. Lovecraft

H. P. Lovecraft is often cited as an influence by American writers of uncanny fiction. This book knocked me sideways when I read it – it is so strangely written. The opening passages are particularly good. As with Poe (and Robert E. Howard, another writer, like Lovecraft, whose work graced the pages of pulp magazines in the 1930s) there is something deranged – almost hysterical – about the prose style itself. But I mean that in a good way.

CREATIVE TIPS FOR WRITING
CREEPY STORIES

The first thing is your work environment. This has to be just right. It should be gloomy, of course, but not enough people appreciate the importance of dankness in the creative process. I myself work in a crypt by the light of a single flickering candle.

There must be no computer, phone or iAnything, naturally. Did Edgar Allan Poe tweet? Did M. R. James check Facebook every ten minutes? No, no, no. Horror must be written by hand, alone, undisturbed (at least by the living).

I favour a quill pen myself and find that only a feather from a raven will do. I tried a goose feather once, but nevermore.

For an inkwell, I use the hollowed out human skull of a man hanged at Tyburn for murder in 1725. But really any skull will do.

Actually, much of that isn't strictly speaking true.

I write creepy stories the same way I write everything else. First of all I fill notebooks with ideas. There is a tip right there – always carry a notebook. Always. And try to do a better job than me in remembering where you last put it.

The ideas in the notebooks can range from a whole concept for a story, to a snatch of dialogue or the solution to a problem that has been bugging me for weeks.

These notes then turn into pages on my computer – all right, yes, I do use a computer – and these pages find their way into folders that may become books.

But these 'ideas' I scribble in my notebooks for creepy stories are often ideas for endings. Often the work is in how you get to that ending, and how you stop your reader from guessing where you are headed. Ideas are obviously important, but they are only the start and they are never enough – however good – to carry a story on their own.

Like a good joke, a good piece of horror fiction is all about the way it's told. Be prepared to rework and rework it until it flows naturally. Horror is a particularly contrived area of fiction, but it must not seem like that to the reader. You must make the unbelievable believable. And that takes time and a lot of effort.

Obviously – as with all writing – it's a good idea to read things by other writers you feel are good at it and see if you can figure out what it is they are doing that works so well. Read some Edgar Allan

Poe. Or some Shirley Jackson. Or see if you can come up with anything half as creepy as *The Family of the Vourdalak* by Tolstoy. Watch *The Innocents* . . . or *The Haunting* (the 1963 original of course).

But I'm showing my prejudices here. Horror is a very wide genre and I am talking mainly about the understated wing – the dark one, with creaking floorboards and something twitching and scratching in the shadows.

There is a much more bloody face to horror of course. But I am not especially interested in gore as the punchline to a story, either in a book or in a movie. Gore has its place – and gory things do happen in my stories – but I'm looking for something else usually as a reader and a writer.

I might not know what it is when I start out, but I'll recognise it when it slithers towards me.

A CONVERSATION WITH
THE AUTHOR

How would you describe your Tales of Terror *collections to potential readers?*

The Tales of Terror are collections of short creepy tales, but they are told by a different storyteller in each book. During the course of each of the books, we learn about the storyteller and about the listeners. Each of the books is set in the past – in the Victorian and Edwardian era that is the setting for so many classic English ghost stories.

What was the original inspiration behind these terrifying tales?

There were lots of different inspirations, but more than anything they came out of my love of short uncanny fiction – ghost stories, weird tales, sci-fi, horror. I wondered if I could write psychological chillers for a young readership. I wanted to see if kids today would like the kind of stories I liked when I was thirteen or fourteen or so.

You've added bonus stories to the back of each of the Tales of Terror *that bring all three books together. Were these difficult to write?*

It was actually a lot of fun to return to those books and those characters after writing a couple of novels. I am really pleased with the way the stories have worked out. I was determined that we shouldn't just tack a story on to the end. I wanted the books to be better for the addition, and I think they are. The new sections link the books together in a way that did not happen before.

Do you see Uncle Montague as a creepy character? Did you have fun creating him and is he based on anyone you know?

Uncle Montague gets his name from M. R. James – Montague Rhodes James – but as I wrote about him I had those greats of horror movies in mind: people like Peter Cushing, Vincent Price, John Carradine and Boris Karloff. Roald Dahl was in there too, I suppose, with his introductions to his *Tales of the Unexpected* television programmes.

Some people think that horror writers must be a little weird to come up with their stories. Would you agree with them?

Yes. It is weird. But writing is a weird occupation whatever you write. One of the strongest impulses for me to try to get published was that I kept thinking how weird it was to be keeping notebooks full of stories when I was not (then) a published writer.

Your next book, Mister Creecher, *is a twist on the Frankenstein story. Could you tell us a little bit more about it and the inspiration behind it?*

Ever since I read the book in my teens, I was fascinated by the fact that Frankenstein, his friend Clerval and the creature all come to Britain, going on a tour through London and Oxford, up into the Lakes and eventually to Scotland and the Orkney Islands (where Frankenstein will build – and then destroy – a mate for his creation). Mary Shelley whizzes through this journey in a few paragraphs, but I wanted to zoom in on the potential of having that huge, angry, vengeful monster loose in the England of 1818. *Mister Creecher* imagines a meeting between Frankenstein's creature and a young street thief in Regency London and charts the strange and dangerous bond that develops between them as they leave London and head north.

MORE SPINE-CHILLING STORIES
FROM CHRIS PRIESTLEY

'Wonderfully macabre and beautifully
crafted horror stories'
Chris Riddell

 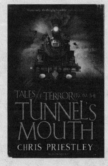 

'Guaranteed to give you nightmares'
Observer

HAUNTING BOOKSHOPS NOW

NEW FROM
THE MASTER OF THE MACABRE

Can a monster and a boy ever really be friends?

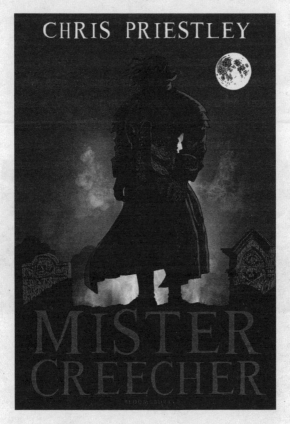

Find out in this fantastically frightening gothic novel

OUT NOW